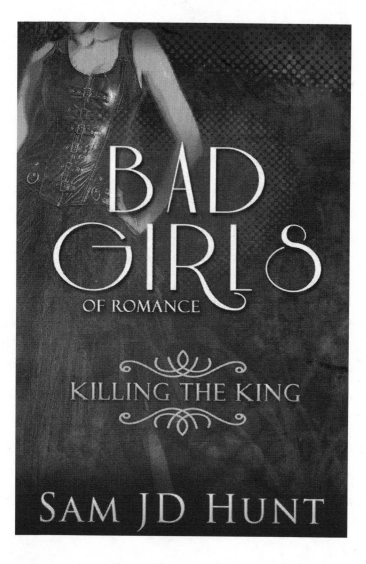

BAD GIRLS
OF ROMANCE

KILLING THE KING

SAM JD HUNT

KILLING THE KING

SAM JD HUNT

~

Forgive me Father, for I am about to sin.

As spring melts into the hottest summer I've ever known, my love for my new parish priest fuels a rebellion deep in my soul that no man dare tame. Once unleashed, not even the all-powerful King of England can contain the force that I will become.

It's time for an unholy war, and my forbidden lover and I will fight to the death before we let our fire be blown out.

Can a love born in hell ever make it to heaven?
Will a soul destined to kill ever truly live?

~

Take me to church
I'll worship like a dog at the shrine of your lies
I'll tell you my sins and you can sharpen your knife
Offer me that deathless death
Good God, let me give you my life. – Hozier

PART I
WORTHINGTON, EAST ANGLIA, ENGLAND

Summer, 1524

THERESA "TESS" DARBY

"Hurry up Tess," my mother called to me. "We'll be late for church."

I hated church and all other things regarding village life. But, as much as I might try, I doubted I'd get out of going to mass that particular day. There was a new priest in town.

I tossed my dress on over my smock, smoothed my hair, and wiped my face.

"Coming," I screamed, running through the door and down the lane.

Father was furious when I caught up to them. He spun on his heel and raged at me. "Stupid girl! Always late." With the smack of his large hand, I struggled to stay upright. I wasn't about to give him the satisfaction of seeing me fall. Besides, I had my new dress on.

My mother stared at him in disdain, but didn't dare speak up.

"Are you next?" he threatened her. She said nothing, but I knew she was making note of it in her always-plotting head. One day, I knew, she would have the final say. But today, we had to do our best to stay out of the path of his fist, or worse.

Of course when we finally arrived, it was packed. The stone church was always full because no one dared displease the Lord lest you get sweating sickness or the dreaded plague. But that day, it was nearly standing room only. Everyone in the area traveled to Worthington to see the man that was replacing the disgraced Father Dunham.

I however, could not care any less. I studied my fingertips, trying to avoid the lustful eyes of John the Brewer several pews away. He always stared at me like I was a piece of meat he wanted to eat. Mother pinched me and told me to pay attention as the dark-clothed figure made his way to the pulpit.

As he looked up at us, I was suddenly *very* interested. When he spoke the rote words of the liturgy, his voice was so smooth and wondrous that I pinched my thighs together.

I couldn't pry my eyes off of the new priest, Father Edmond Gregory. Dark wavy hair that cascaded to his shoulders, pale hazel eyes, full lips, and a broad nose; he was the loveliest thing the entire congregation had ever seen.

By the time I was in front of him receiving the wine and the host, I was sure I was in love. And then, with the dry wafer on my tongue, it happened. He smiled at me! I'd never seen a man of the cloth be anything but dour.

I was frozen in front of him like a statue. And he continued to smile, until finally with a wink he nodded for me to move on.

Later, during our evening meal, my father raged against the new priest.

"I don't know, he seems to breathe new life into the church," my mother argued.

"Don't be daft, Eleanor," he snapped. "He's nothing but a damnable member of the gentry. The son of the Lord Gregory doesn't belong here! Clearly he's committed a sin most foul to be sent to this hell. Someone of his birth would normally be in front of a large cathedral in London or at least Cambridge."

"His sin can't be as lecherous as that of our last priest at least," my younger sister added, risking a smack from my father. Luckily, he was out of energy and merely finished his ale and left for the tavern.

When we were alone, my mother looked to me. "Jacob Tanner asked about you after service today."

"I don't want to marry a tanner! They are always stained and foul-smelling."

"Jacob is a decent man, and if you wait much longer the pickings will be slim."

"He's just so…ordinary!"

"Who doth thou desire to wed, my Princess?" my mother asked, her sarcasm clear. We both knew I had no choice in whom I would marry. Women in the sixteenth century had very little say in such matters. To father, I was another mouth to feed and was well beyond the age most girls were married off.

With a luscious grin, I answered her question. "Father Gregory, I'll take *him*."

I was accustomed to my father's rough hand; my mother was far gentler. That afternoon, however, my blasphemous comment earned me a hard hit to my ear.

~

I saw him the next day. He was walking through the market stalls, but buying nothing. I followed him, careful not to draw attention to myself. When he turned a corner, I hurried up to catch a longer glance, but he was gone.

I looked around the market seeking his fine face when he spoke behind me.

"It seems I have a shadow."

I turned, my face redder than Jacob the Tanner's hands. "Father, no, I was, er, I simply need to buy…" I couldn't think of anything I could possibly be shopping for.

He smiled wide. "I am glad for the company, dear Theresa. Shall we find some tallow for the church's candles?"

Father Gregory remembered my name!

"Everyone calls me Tess."

"Then Tess it will be. Everyone calls me Father Gregory, unfortunately." And then it happened. He laughed! *A young, handsome priest who laughs and smiles,* I thought. I was smitten, and I could not get enough of him.

∼

We spent all afternoon wandering the town, for much longer than I was allowed to be away. I knew by dusk I'd earn a beating for my impertinence, but I didn't care. I'd have done anything to spend one more second with him.

But far too soon he looked at the horizon and said, "It's getting dark. You'd best be heading home."

I frowned, never wanting the day to end.

"But listen, Tess, I'll let you in on a secret."

"A secret!"

"Yes, it's about why I'm here. I chose Worthington as an experiment for a study I'm doing. I intend to make my ministry teaching, especially reading. And, I plan to include *everyone.*"

"Not women," I argued.

He leaned in close, and in my ear said the words I'd remember for the rest of my life. "*Especially* women."

"Oh!" was all I could think to say. Then, like a silly braggart, blurted out, "But I can already read!"

Immediately embarrassed, I covered my mouth with my hand. My boldness often got me into trouble.

"That's wonderful!" He glanced at the setting sun again. "If you can get away, come to the church tomorrow and perhaps we'll begin. If you know of others who want to learn, young or old, pass the word."

"I will," I said as I turned to walk home.

～

"No." That was all father said the next day when I asked him if I could attend Father Gregory's classes. "I forbid it."

"But grandfather taught me to read, and if I could possibly do sums I would be a better wife for a tradesman, surely."

"Your grandfather was a fool. Educated women are dangerous women. Oh, and Tess, stay far away from that lecherous priest or I'll ring your neck like a chicken."

But of course I didn't listen. I rarely did. The very next afternoon, I sat on a bench at my parish church and showed Father Gregory that I could read some of the Latin words in his Bible.

"I'm astonished!" he admitted. "I doubt any of the men in the village can do that."

"They can't," I boasted. "Most cannot read even English, nor do they care to."

He rested his hand on top of mine, sending a tremor through my body. "You are special, Tess Darby," he said. "There are great things in store for you."

I floated on air at his touch, but too soon he pulled his hand away.

"You must tell no one that I allowed you to read the Bible," he warned.

I shook my head, "No! Not a word." We both knew how scandalous the idea of anyone other than clergy reading the holy text was.

7

~

I wasn't his only student, but I was the only girl. The boys he taught separately, and he confided in me that none lasted very long. Most were farmers, and had little ambition beyond the daily drudgery that they knew.

"The boys, it seems they just come out of curiosity, and then quickly find it too hard," he said to me one rainy afternoon.

"Oh Father, I love the learning! I dream of one day leaving this place. I want to see things, *do* things, but I'm trapped. My father is seeking a husband for me."

His eyes met mine, and I melted like the candles above the altar.

"I'd think it would be easy to find a husband for one such as you. Beautiful, smart, and..." Then he caught himself, and his eyes left mine.

"They all find me different. None of the men in this town seem to want *different*."

"No, I suppose not," he said coldly. "It's time for you to go. Your parents will wonder where you are."

But I hesitated, not wanting the day to end. I stood up and leaned in close, "They don't care as long as my chores are done. I can stay—we can start on the new French verb tense you were going to teach me."

And then it happened. A simple gesture, but it happened. Father Gregory stroked my cheek. It was only brief, and he quickly pulled back from my skin as if he'd been struck. "No, tomorrow. French, yes, of course. Goodnight, Tess."

In a flurry, he fled into the bowels of the church before I'd even started toward the door.

When I returned the next day after my work in the field was done, he was different. Something had changed between us.

"Father, did I do something wrong? I know French doesn't come naturally to me, but I shall try harder."

He bit his lip and glanced around the empty sanctuary.

"No, it's not you. Slide over and we'll start the grammar."

"Oh, thank you!" I said, squeezing his hand.

Once again he pulled his hand from mine as if branded by a hot iron. "I-I'm sorry, I didn't mean to offend you. I just thought—"

"You're a woman, Tess. Stop acting like a child."

I never touched him again, and my studies continued as usual until one day, it all changed.

~

It happened one afternoon during the third week of my studies. Father Gregory was trying to teach me geometry. Languages were my strength, but I was fascinated with angles and architecture.

We were in the upper reaches of the church, dark and dusty, when he pointed to the massive Norman arch and asked me why there was strength in the structure.

I held up my hand to trace the shape in the air, and then it happened.

In the deep darkness of the old building, our fingertips met. I felt the force between us erupt, like the sizzle of a wet finger on a hot branding iron. It was a sensation so magical that it had to be ours alone.

"Father, I feel faint."

"As do I," he said. "As do I."

Neither of us moved as the energy flowed through us.

When his eyes met mine, I knew I loved him.

"This feeling is so new to me!" I blurted out.

His eyes lit up as he wrapped his warm hand around mine. "It is older than time."

"Do you feel it too?" I could barely contain my joy.

He let go of my hand as darkness floated across his face. "Sadly, yes."

"Sadly? I feel as if I could fly!"

"Tess, this can go no further."

"Oh Father, but it must!"

He shook his head and sat down on the cold floor of the attic. "I am not free. And, even if I were free to marry, my family would never allow me to wed a peasant. It would be an arranged marriage for money, or for power, or most likely, for both."

"Then we will not marry," I said naively. "We will merely continue to love one another as I learn." I smiled wide, my mind made up.

He nodded and forced a smile across his lips. "It'll be our secret, then."

"Yes! We shall love in the shadows." I couldn't get past the fact that this gorgeous man might care for me. Back then, the reality of how dire the situation was never crossed my innocent mind.

FATHER EDMOND GREGORY

I knew she was special the first time I placed the host on her tongue. It wasn't that she was pretty – not only pretty, but seriously beautiful. I'd had scores of beautiful women. It was something more. A connection, the knowing look of a soul so rare that it must be for a purpose. But that wasn't really enough to derail me from my mission in Worthington. Not in the beginning, anyway.

I'd been sent to the small village to atone for a sin. My uncle was the powerful Bishop of Cambridge, Reginald Gregory, and when damaging whispers started circling about my time in seminary, he decided to move me someplace quiet. Someplace where the church wouldn't notice me.

If only he'd known how far-reaching that mindless decision would prove to be. If only he'd known then the impact that Tess Darby would have on us all.

When she started her studies with me, I grew to love her. Not just want her, but love her deeply as I'd never loved. She was far younger than me, and far more innocent, but Tess was well past marrying age. And my lovely student was bril-

11

liant – the smartest pupil I'd ever had. Like a sponge she learned, like one so hungry for knowledge that she'd starve to death if her mind couldn't continue to be fed.

I didn't mean to let it happen. The stroke of a cheek, the touch of a hand, our legs pressed together in the pew while she studied philosophy – our desire grew, day by day. By the time I saw her undressed one afternoon, I was already on fire with love for her.

It wasn't a classic David and Bathsheba moment, but like the Biblical lovers, watching Tess bathe was when our fall from grace began. Her nearly naked body was the most beautiful vision I'd ever seen.

It started innocently enough. That summer was hot, the hottest we'd known in the middle of England in years. Suffocating under my heavy clerical robes, one afternoon I'd had enough. Priest or not, I was determined to find the one thing that could cool me down – water. Running water, to be more specific.

Earlier that afternoon, one of my parishioners, Abner Stone, told me of a place out amongst the forest of trees to the east of his large farm. "No one ever goes there, Father, just my boys and me. You're welcome to cool down there in peace."

So after my final service of the day, I mounted my trusty horse and rode out of the stifling town toward the cool shade of the tall trees. Robe-free in the privacy of the lush green canopy, I stripped as far down as I dared.

But when I finally reached the stream, there was someone else already there. Quieting my horse, I knelt low under the cover of the tall reeds. It was the woman I could not stop thinking about. The one my soul yearned for; the bright, witty girl I'd watched blossom into a woman. Tess Darby, the one I could never have. When our fingers met the day prior, I knew that what flowed between us was forbidden, and pure trouble.

But still, I could not keep my eyes off of her. She wasn't naked. Even more maddening, she was covered only by the thin cotton of her threadbare shift. The effect of seeing her in her most intimate clothes, that nearest to her skin, was far more erotic than if I'd been witness to her complete nudity.

Her hair was down, free of the heavy hood that hid it from view in public. A ray of sunlight caught her golden hair, and as she raised her hands to stretch, she appeared to be an angel descending briefly from heaven to grace this harsh world with her glory.

When she dipped down into the cool water and reemerged, it was as if all of heaven had fallen to earth. Her gown was wet, and the thin white cotton grew transparent. The curve of her thigh, the dark triangle where I longed to be, her kissable pink nipples were all there, all of her glory in front of me. I knew if I stayed one more minute, I'd have her in my arms; I'd have her underneath me. Women I'd had plenty of, but this one I knew was forbidden. I turned to go.

In silence, I walked my horse from the stream. Until, echoing through the trees, I heard her scream in the distance. Running back, I couldn't find her. The stream was empty, but her dress lay on the rocks where she'd been washing it.

"Tess!"

Only a muffled sound came back in return. *Had she drown?*

I rushed into the water, but then I heard the sound of her voice coming from a thicket of dense bushes. "You'll do nothing when I cut off your manhood!"

I followed the sound, and found Richard Stone, one of my less-talented students, on top of a wet and naked Tess. "Get off of her, or I'll run you through!" Of course I didn't actually have a weapon of any kind on me, and the bully Richard was twice my size. But to me, those details were meaningless.

"Why don't you go pray while I fornicate with this whore," he said.

"I warned you once," Tess said from beneath him. Before I could get to them, the behemoth attacker shrieked like a dying mouse. He rolled off of Tess, clawing at his vest as if a swarm of bees had suddenly entered.

Tess was on top of him in seconds, a small dagger in her right hand. "More? You said you wanted to play, did you not?" She stabbed him again, a little lower.

"I'll kill you!"

Her blade went to his throat, to his very jugular. "You'll die after I stuff your cock and balls into your evil mouth!"

"Tess, don't do this thing." In truth, I'd have enjoyed watching that rapist die. But the cover-up would have been far too risky. I was supposed to be avoiding attention, after all.

"Father!" She looked to me, the tip of her blade at the man's jugular.

"It's done, my child." I took a few more steps toward them. "Let him go, and it will all be well."

Her blade left his throat, but in one final defiance, she sliced two shallow lines across his bloated cheeks. "That's so you don't forget, Richard Stone."

"You'll pay!" the coward shouted as he ran away.

Tess sat in the grass, her bloody blade at her side. "Are you hurt?" I asked.

She shook her head. "I'd just like to go home now."

~

The next day, she sat in my confession booth.

"Tess? You asked to meet me here." She'd been silent for several long minutes.

"I-I would have killed him yesterday, Father."

"I know."

"If you hadn't stopped me…"

"Here's my confession, my child. I didn't want to stop you. In another time, another place, I'd have killed him myself."

She gasped. "But surely I've committed a grave sin."

"You've done no wrong. He was the attacker."

"Sometimes I can't control myself."

I was intrigued; suddenly feeling like Worthington wasn't such a random choice of parishes after all. Maybe I was there for a reason; maybe I was there for her. "Do you always carry a dagger?"

"Yes. Once when I was a child of five, I was attacked by a wild boar. By the time my incompetent father found me, I'd carved the thing up for dinner."

"Your attacker was on top of you, far heavier than us both combined. How did you disable him?"

"Easy. It's all about knowing where to stick the blade."

"And you learned that by…?"

"By watching. And practicing."

"I see." My mind was racing; beautiful, brilliant, *and* deadly.

She interrupted my thoughts. "Father Gregory, am I from hell? Many say I am *other*, that I am not of God."

"You, my beautiful dear, are the nearest to heaven I've ever been. Go, and sin no more. Unless you need to."

∼

After that day, her studies continued in secret, but the

dynamic between us had intensified. Day after day we sat, our legs touching, our hands brushing one another, as she poured through all of the books I owned. One day, when the hour grew late, I stood up and stretched. Tess was by my side, and without meaning to, we locked into a deep embrace.

"We shouldn't," I said, the smell of her intoxicating me.

"We must. Can we not love in secret?"

"I want to, you know that. But it's dangerous. Forbidden."

"Surely there must be a way!"

"Sweet Tess, go home. Perhaps I'll speak to my uncle. If he could find a place for you in Cambridge, then perhaps there's a chance."

"Father would never agree. He's cruel, bitter."

I held her close, despite the danger. There had to be a way to save her.

Feeling hopeful, we parted. But what I didn't know was that we were being watched.

The very next evening, the vile man accosted me in the empty nave. "I know what's been going on with my daughter," he hissed into my ear, the stink of his breath turning my stomach.

"You know nothing, evil man." I turned to see the dark face of George Darby, my beloved Tess' father, inches from my own.

"I've seen it!" he howled like a rabid dog.

The man towered over me like a giant, his massive chest heaving from his anger. I willed myself to be calm, to think. Calmness was a great advantage over the anger fueled. Tess had her knife skills, but my biggest talent was the ability to always remain in control of emotion.

"You've seen nothing," I said slowly. "You are letting Satan fill your weak mind with your own sinful thoughts."

"If you want my daughter, Father, you'll have to pay," he said through clenched teeth.

"Want? *Your* daughter?" I shook my head. "I've taught her to read Latin, a little bit of mathematics, nothing more."

"*That* in itself is sin! Proof that you are not holy!" He spat the words out, foul spittle coating his twitching lips.

"Who are *you*, George Darby, the lowly seller of wool, to question the agent of God himself?"

"I'm-I'm, I know what I saw! Abner Stone was right about the two of you."

I took a deep breath. My hope had been to simply control this ignorant man's mind, but his anger was far too great. He was also full of greed, which was far more powerful than anger.

"You saw nothing."

"I saw your arms around her waist," he spat. "I saw her lean her tender parts into yours! You sin, Father!" He stepped toward me, his horrible breath causing me to grimace.

"So what?" I said with a shoulder shrug.

"So what? *So* you will pay me! Have her, defile her, do whatever – but I will have gold for it."

I shook my head. "You, stupid man, will go home and have *nothing*. You will *say* nothing. Do you understand?"

The massive brute then made an error that, if he were not her father, would have proven fatal. George the Wooler lunged, his fists moving to strike at me like a baited bear.

In seconds, my right hand reached up toward his neck. With the skills taught to me by the master, he was frozen with one squeeze of my agile fingers. He couldn't move.

"You dare attack the servant of God in His own house?"

He blinked but had no control of his monstrous body.

"I could kill you right now, and you'd go straight to the fires of hell."

There was terror in his dark eyes. Despite his sacrilege, the silly man believed all the myth of heaven and hell.

"Never, ever, threaten me again. Next time my hand

touches you, it'll be the last." I withdrew from the secret nerve that I'd used to incapacitate him.

He slumped to the floor. "Magic!" he said.

"No, foolish man. It is a miracle of God."

He made the sign of the cross as I walked away.

TESS

❧

I saw the entire thing.

It started earlier that day, when I was helping mother churn the milk into butter. My horrible father burst through the thin door shouting, "Whore!"

We both looked at him, unsure which of us was being called that foul word.

"George, what is this about? Have some ale," my mother said calmly.

"Your daughter is a whore! I saw her rubbing all over that heretic, Father Gregory!"

My mother made the sign of the cross, infuriating him even further. "Now, now, George, surely you are mistaken."

"It was in the very house of God! In front of the altar!"

She looked to me, her lips pursing. I gave her a quick shrug; I had no explanation. After my Latin lesson, I rose to leave and somehow, without our ability to stop it, the magical pull we shared drew our bodies together.

We'd stood like that for endless minutes, his arms around my waist, until as if awakening from a spell he'd whispered for me to go. The incident was in the main sanctuary of the great stone church, anyone could have seen us.

And, despite my father's rage, I didn't regret one second of it.

"Perhaps it is a good thing," my mother said with a wink.

"A good thing?" we yelled in unison, both of us astounded at my mother's level of cunning.

"If the *rich* priest would like to take certain liberties with our innocent, maiden daughter, then perhaps he could pay."

My father looked to me with an evil grin. "If this doesn't work, I'm coming back to beat both of you to a pulp."

So while my mother ground the roots and mushrooms she would need to subdue him later, I followed Father in the shadows. I watched as he entered the church and his ultimate confrontation with the man I loved.

My father was a dangerous man; I'd seen him use his huge fists to pummel a man to death when I was a mere child. The monster I'd been born to weighed nearly twice that of my beloved Father Gregory, and there was no way I was going to let that beast harm the man I loved.

One of the blades that I always had hidden in my skirts was in my right hand. I was ready to do whatever it took to stop my wife-beating, child-abusing, scourge of a father.

But I didn't need to. To my amazement, Father Gregory had skills that even surpassed my own. I watched as he used a sort of mystical power to subdue my father. Despite the difference in size, my love had been in total control.

Later, long after it was all over, I approached Father Gregory in the darkness of the courtyard. "How'd you do that?"

"Do what, Tess?"

I drew close to him, but he reminded me with the raise of his hand that we were outdoors, in public. "You froze him as if he'd fallen in the coldest ice!"

His finger went to his lips, reminding me to be quiet. "How did you do that?" I repeated.

"It's not magic, my dear girl; it's simple anatomy. A friar taught me years ago."

"Would you teach me?" The blade was my friend, but I could think of all kinds of uses for Father Gregory's less bloody method.

He nodded. "I will try. But for now, you need to go home. Will your father try to harm you?"

I shook my head. "No, Mother made him that special tea that makes him sleep for days."

He laughed out loud, and briefly took my hands in his. "Sleep well, sweet Tess. It might be best if you avoid this place for a week or so until he cools down."

"I will suffer the greatest loss in not seeing you," I whined.

"I shall miss you, but be good and stay out of trouble."

We both knew I wouldn't.

~

I didn't get the chance to see Father Gregory again before the worst happened. My father had the last laugh, and his revenge was far crueler than I could have imagined.

John the Brewer's wife died that Tuesday, and within days he had contracted with Father to have me. He'd been through *several* young wives. I pouted, I cried, I stamped my feet like a baby mule, but to no avail. I was to either marry as my father demanded, or be put out to starve, or worse.

Heartbroken, I went to Father Gregory.

He stared out the stained glass window without a word.

"Please, I need guidance."

He sighed and wrapped his arms around his chest. "I have no guidance. Only that this earth is a terrible place, and even more horrid for the poor and, as always, the *female*."

Leaving me alone on a pew, he fled with the slamming of the door.

That very Sunday, my beloved priest glanced at the paper and nodded. My stomach turned as he read it aloud. When the yellow-rimmed eyes of John the Brewer turned toward me from across the congregation, I knew I would be sick.

I ran from the mass, the fateful words of the marriage banns echoing behind me. As my stomach emptied into the hedges, the reality of my fate hit me like a kick to the gut.

I'd been betrothed to marry the old, the ugly, the violent John Brewer.

"I'm sorry, Tess," a voice said from behind me.

"Jacob, thank you."

He handed me a cloth to clean my lips. "I asked him for you, you know. He refused."

My mother had urged me to marry Jacob the Tanner for as long as I could remember. Father not agreeing was a surprise.

"Why did he object?"

"At first, I assumed it was because you did not want me. Later I learned from your mother that it was because I wasn't cruel enough."

I shook in terror. "Shall I die at the hand of my husband, Jacob Tanner?"

"I hope not, Tess. You are the only light in my life, even if I must enjoy your glow from afar. Please know *I* never would have hurt you."

He left me without another word, his heart as shattered as my own.

～

I appealed to my mother the very next day, but she sighed as she poured the tea. "There's nothing I can do."

"But why? Can you not whip up a potion to change his mind?"

I was desperate, but she merely shook her head. "It doesn't work like that, child."

"Find another match," I begged. "Jacob the Tanner, you like him."

"That ship has long since sailed."

"Anyone!" I begged.

She reached for her tea. "Tess, you are past marrying age and many rumor that you are not a maid."

"I am untouched!"

"Nonetheless, there's an exoticness about you that causes them to doubt. Farmer Stone's son has even come just short of accusing you of witchcraft."

"I'm not the one with the potions," I argued, glancing toward the various roots on her mantle.

"Careful, girl," she warned. "I may be one of the few friends you have left."

I sat down and sipped my tea. "The brewer is too old and he's already had *three* wives. The way he looks at me..." I shivered at the thought.

"It cannot be helped. We are but mere women, and John has ample means to take you as a wife. The match will be good for your father. The brewer has even offered to apprentice your youngest brother into his trade. Wool will not last forever, and it will be good to have something more to rely on."

Her words made sense, but we all knew the real reason I was being given to that terrible man. "This is revenge, nothing more."

She nodded. "Yes. But you brought this upon yourselves, and now, I fear, you will have to pay for it."

"What should I do, Mother?"

"Be obedient, be quiet. Bide your time and wait it out."

~

"Ah, if it isn't my sweet wife!"

I'd been shopping in the market when his disgusting hands groped at me, pulling my dress low to expose my breasts further.

"I'm not your wife. Not yet." My voice was cold, my lips in a sneer.

"You may as well be." He clawed at me again, my right hand drifting toward my blade. *I could kill him with one jab*, I thought.

"So very virginal, aren't you? Well I've heard otherwise and I want to see for myself before I pledge my troth." He moved closer, one hand on the growing bulge in his trousers and the other grasping at my breast.

When he pinched my nipple so hard I could bear it no more, I drew my blade.

And then I heard him from behind us. "John, surely this is improper behavior. I cannot condone it."

The horrible demon released my flesh as he turned to our priest.

"Father, er, I…"

"You what?"

"I lost my senses. This is my bride, and I was simply…"

"God frowns upon this. See not this maid again until your wedding day."

John was stammering. He was a foul, cruel man, but he was pious and feared the wrath of God.

"Yes, Father."

"I'll see you in confession," Father Gregory said. "Now."

John turned and nearly ran from us, heading toward the church.

"Thank you," I said, moving to embrace him.

He pulled back. "No, no more of that. That is done."

My eyes brimmed with tears. "But, it's you that I want to—"

He turned to walk away, and over his shoulder sadly said, "May God have mercy on us all."

EDMOND

*H*er pale blue eyes, her golden hair peeking out from under her hood, that ivory skin that defied her time laboring in the fields... I could not stop thinking about Tess Darby. The thought of her with that monster maddened me; I'd come close to ending the whole thing. And yet I waited. This was her battle, her war, and I knew I mustn't decide for her.

The week after I'd first read her marriage banns, she came to me after mass. Tears brimmed her golden eyelashes as she made her request. It broke my heart, but I knew I could not do the thing she asked of me.

"Please, Father," she nearly begged. "I trust you."

That was exactly the reason I couldn't grant her request. That, and of course, the fact that I was madly in love with her. "It's impossible, my child. I'm sorry."

"If you won't perform the marriage rite, then who will? Will it stop the wedding?" It hurt to see the hope on her face. If only I could do as she wished, if only I could stop the marriage. But I had no power to do that. She belonged to her

26

father, to do with as he pleased as if she were one of his sheep in the field.

My heart humped in my chest. I longed to touch her, to embrace her. "My uncle the bishop is coming from Cambridge, Tess. A huge honor, I assure you. All of the village girls will be jealous that you were married by the famous Bishop Reginald Gregory."

"But I want *you*," she whined, biting her lower lip.

And I you, more than I can ever dream of, I thought. "My dearest, you know you are special to me."

She nodded, wiping the tears from her cheek.

As much as I wanted to be near her, I knew I could never bear to perform the ceremony. To stand there and give her to another, I'd never be able to do it.

Even if it were a good man I could not, but to my horror the man chosen for her was not a good man. He was a monster. Even worse, he was a pious monster who confessed his evil deeds to his parish priest - me. I wanted to strangle him with my bare hands, and now he was to have my Tess.

~

The following Sunday, I was in my uncle's chambers at the great cathedral in Cambridge when he returned from Worthington.

"Is it done? The marriage?" My heart pounded in my chest.

"Yes," he said.

I thought I was going to be sick. Grasping the table, I stared at him.

My uncle, the great Bishop of Cambridge, refilled my glass with the finest wine from France as he shook his head at me. "Get over her, Edmond."

More wine was the last thing I needed that day – I'd been drinking since dawn.

"Don't be ridiculous, Uncle."

Several slurps later, my glass was empty again. He refilled it with a frown. "Edmond, this assignment is temporary. I need you to be a lowly priest for merely a few months longer and I can put your name in for one of the bigger priories. This girl, this peasant, isn't part of the plan."

"You've had three mistresses and eleven illegitimate children," I said.

"Beside the point." He waved his hand as if swatting at a fly. "You cannot pine for this girl. Fornicate with all the women you want, procreate until you fill England with your bastard spawn, but stay away from Tess Brewer."

"*Brewer*," I spat.

"Yes, Edmond, she is now the wife of John the Brewer. Tess Brewer, a married woman in your parish. Now move on."

"She's brilliant, did you know that? She can do sums better than any merchant I've seen, and her Latin in just a year rivals that of most cardinals—"

"Stop! That is precisely why you may not have her. She is dangerous; I saw it in her eyes. She's trouble and she will bring you down. She will bring us *all* down, I fear. Hell hath no fury like a thinking woman."

"That's not the quote, and he is beneath her," I snapped with the impertinence of a child.

"I don't care, as long as she is *not* beneath *you*."

"That man is horrible, cruel. I'm his confessor, I know."

"Not your concern, *Father Gregory*. Do I need to have you reassigned?"

"No," I answered. I knew he would do it, and I couldn't stand the idea of not seeing her, not protecting her.

"Her husband has demanded that her studies with you at the church cease at once."

"Of course," I nodded. I knew that one was coming. Her father had never allowed her learning, and I was sure her new primitive husband would be even less enthusiastic about an educated woman.

"And if he hurts her? I mean seriously, like he did his last wife?"

"Then you are to do nothing."

My mind raced for answers, but there weren't any. "How very Christian," I muttered, refilling my wine glass, praying for numbness to take away the pain.

"Edmond, I'm not heartless. I know what it's like to love the forbidden; to want what one cannot have. But this girl, this *woman*, there's something about her that isn't holy. She's different."

"She's perfect." I stared into my glass, visions of her eyes dancing in the reflection.

"You must avoid Tess Darby at all costs."

"Tess *Brewer*," I growled.

My uncle was feared and always, always obeyed. Except, of course, we both knew that in this matter I would be disobedient. What we didn't know then was how the force of my rebellion or my love for Tess, and Sister Elizabeth after her, would shake the known world to its very core.

~

As harsh as the pain was, I knew I couldn't stay away from her forever. The following Sunday, I was once again in the pulpit. My eyes scanned the congregation for her, but she wasn't there.

I fumbled through mass, my mind only on her.

Afterward, in the churchyard, I was able to approach her mother. "I pray that all is well within your family?" I tried to sound merely polite, but we both knew it was more.

"Of course, Father. We did regret your absence at Tess' wedding." Her eyes narrowed at me.

"Yes, but it could not be helped. I had pressing business in Cambridge."

"Pressing business," she repeated with drawn lips.

"I trust the bishop performing the ceremony was a great honor?"

She nodded. "Of course."

Eleanor Darby had the gift of sight, and we both knew it. Against my better judgment, I couldn't help but ask. "And your daughter? Is she well in her new union?"

Her eyes darkened and she said in a near-whisper, "What do you think?"

The following week, Tess was in the congregation with her husband. Over communion, our eyes met. I knew then that she wasn't angry with me. An ugly bruise marred her perfect cheek, and I wanted to strangle John the Brewer right there in my very own church.

After that, I saw her only at church, her devotion to her prayers far more dedicated than they had been before her nightmare of a marriage.

Her confession also came weekly, but was usually the benign chattering of a young woman. Only after she'd been married for a while did her tone darken. Still, she never told me of her husband's cruelty. I, however, not only heard *his* confessions, but I'd been briefly privy to those of his former wife.

His former wife who frequently appeared with broken bones.

His former wife who died while several months pregnant from a fall into their well.

I knew the kind of hell Tess was living in, and I prayed all day, every day that she be spared from his sins. My prayers went unanswered, and one afternoon she sat in my confessional booth and told me everything.

That afternoon, I knew I'd risk all to protect her.

TESS BREWER

*A*fter my marriage, I was never again given a formal lesson. My husband forbade me to be around our priest at all except for confession and mass. Never was I to be alone with *any* other man, and my brutal husband sat outside during what was afforded the only privacy I was allowed: confession.

So that is where I talked to the only friend I had; to the man I secretly loved.

He was distant at first, but as the weeks wore on, Father Gregory became friendlier. Rarely did I actually confess sins. Usually we just talked about life and the secret reading I'd been doing when my husband was gone. Never did I share with my confessor the horror I faced nightly in my own home.

Until one day, I could hide it no longer.

"Forgive me Father, for I have sinned."

The words were so familiar, they usually spilled out of my mouth without a thought. I normally confessed to arguing with my mother, not feeding the chickens, or skipping a prayer or two. But this time was unique. This time I had gravely sinned.

"What sin could you have possibly committed, my child?"

His words were different, his tone on edge. Something had changed, and I felt as if I were about to fall off of a cliff.

"I wished my husband dead."

"Wished?"

"I prayed for him to die. The notion has consumed my every thought."

I heard Father Gregory sigh. I expected shock, eternal damnation. What I heard was relief. "Tess, wishes aren't sins."

"But Father, I prayed for his death. I asked God to…"

"Yes, well, that's the same as a wish. What other mortal sins have you committed this week?"

He leaned in to the metal screen that divided us, so close that I could see a raised eyebrow atop his hazel eye.

I took a deep breath, and despite every fiber inside of me screaming to take my penance and go, I continued.

"The thing is, Father, I want him dead. If God won't grant my prayer, I'll kill him myself."

That got his attention. "Tess, stop," he said, his face touching the screen.

"My mother said I should poison him, but he deserves pain. He deserves to suffer as I have."

Father Gregory took a deep breath from the other side of the confessional. I now had his full attention.

He gulped and said, "Tell me."

"Tell you what?"

"Tell me, Tess, the sins this foul man commits that he deserves to die by your young, innocent hand."

That's when it happened. For an hour, I told Father Gregory everything with more detail than I'd even shared with Mother. From my lips spilled the shameful truth; how John Brewer had raped me, sodomized me, abused my lips, my throat. I revealed how he choked me with his rough hand the entire time he had his way with me, and how afterward he'd punch me, slap me, burn me, and if he was really drunk, he'd cut me with his knife. All of it came forth that afternoon in the sanctity of that holy booth.

When I was finished, I waited. And waited. Father Gregory was silent for what seemed like ages. Had he fallen asleep? Left? Called the magistrate?

I leaned forward, peering into the iron screen. The dark clothed figure of my priest was crumpled into a corner, his face in his perfect hands.

"Father? I'm sorry...I...I shouldn't have said..."

"No, Tess...My God, it's fine, it's just," he said, regaining his composure. "It's just that I hear every manner of horrible thing in this booth. I hear it all. But, this, *to you*, is almost more than I can stand."

"My penance, Father?" I wasn't sure what to do. He was shaken, nervous. "Say five Hail Marys."

"And?" There had to be more. He'd once given me harsher punishment when I confessed to smacking my sister.

"And find a way to get rid of that monster. Follow your mother's advice."

I couldn't move. My backside was frozen to the hard wooden bench as if someone had nailed my skirt there.

I sat motionless until I heard him leave. I couldn't bear the thought of facing him after the things I'd told him. And I hadn't even told him the worst of it. My parish priest didn't know that my husband had made it so that I could never again bear children.

~

Two weeks passed after the confession that would forever change the course of my young life. I couldn't bring myself to face Father Gregory after what I'd told him. Feigning stomach illness, I stayed home from mass and waited for the next explosion from John the Brewer. The explosion never came. Instead, inexplicably, my husband ignored me for those two glorious weeks.

One night, a week after my explosive confession, he came home so drunk he could barely stand. I was sure the peace was over and he'd beat me and do even worse. Instead, he ordered me to the barn. No touching, no hitting, no flames – just a night spent curled up in the hay.

The next morning he was gone before I even milked the cow.

On the way back from the market that afternoon, I stopped by to talk to my mother.

"He hasn't touched me in any way," I confessed as she handed me a cup of ale.

"Are you with child? Could that be it?" She sat across from me at their small wooden table, the only furniture in the house.

"I bled last week," I lied.

"It won't last," she warned.

Shaking her head, she rose and pulled a small pouch from their mantle. "Grind this root and put it in any liquid. Do it soon – they'll think he caught your stomach illness and succumbed to it. Pretend to be ill yourself for several weeks after. When the time of mourning has passed, I'll convince your father to let you marry Jacob the Tanner."

"No, I will never marry again." I knew deep inside that everything had changed. A wife, a mother, a village woman – none of these fates would be mine.

"You must, my daughter. We cannot afford another mouth to feed."

I took the sack of poison from her. "How long will this take? Will it be painful?"

She shook her head. "I know what I'm doing, Tess. It'll be fast, very little pain."

I tucked the poison into the waistband of my skirt. If I needed to take care of John Brewer, I didn't want it to be quick and painless. No, he would suffer as I had.

"They'll be taking the wool to market next week. Your husband has agreed to accompany the boys since your father is unwell." She glanced toward the mantle, where she kept her potions and remedies.

"A week without him will be heaven," I said with a grin.

"Don't blaspheme."

"It will be lovely," I corrected.

"Wait until he returns from Lavenham. His purse will be heavy with coin – he's to be paid a portion of the wool sales, and he'll also sell beer in the market. If you decide to do this thing, Tess, do it then."

And I did wait, mostly because my husband refused to touch me. Without reason, he merely sent me to the barn when he'd return from the tavern. Certainly existence was far more peaceful, but peace wasn't what I desired.

Revenge is what I craved.

Each night, I willed him to do me harm so that I'd have an excuse to carry out my plan. But he did not, and the day came when he left for the wool market in Lavenham with my three younger brothers. Father was too ill to go, and I was sure it had something to do with the dark mark I saw on Mother's cheek.

That evening, after the chores were finished, I curled up wondrously alone in front of my fire. It was long after dark when the knock on my door came. In my evening gown, I quickly pulled a robe around me and reached for my knife as the rapping on the door continued.

"It's me, Edmond," shouted the voice on the other side of the heavy door.

I yanked it open, my trusty weapon abandoned.

"Father Gregory!" I nearly shouted, my mind racing to the fact that he had used his given name seconds prior.

"Call me Edmond tonight. I'm not here as your priest."

"Edmond," I repeated, as if the word was foreign in my mouth.

"Please sit," I said as if this were a normal visit, as if my parish priest ever visited private homes at night except to perform last rites.

"Ale?"

"Do you have wine?"

I shook my head, and with a faint laugh answered, "We peasants can't afford such finery, Father."

"Edmond."

"We lack wine, Edmond, but I assure you my husband brews the best beer in the village."

"I know," he said with a smirk. "I get a tenth of it."

I nodded. The cut of our profits that the church took was stifling.

"He's not here, he went to market with my brothers."

"I know that, too, Tess."

"Oh," was all I could think to say. Suddenly my skin was sweaty, and every nerve within me was pulsing. I was alone at night with a man: with *this* man. With the priest I'd fallen in love with that summer.

I went to pour the ale while he pulled off his heavy tunic. I'd never seen him out of his robe and sash, and the shock of seeing him dressed in normal clothes caused my knees to buckle.

He reached for the cups and gestured for me to sit. "We need to talk, and we haven't much time. I shouldn't be here." He sipped the heady brew and flopped into the chair across from me.

"Is this because I haven't been to church?" Briefly my

innocent mind thought possibly this is what priests do when you miss mass too many times. "My stomach's been unwell."

"Has it?" His right eyebrow went up and his lips pursed.

"No."

He nodded and sipped more of the ale. "The things you told me, I was worried. I thought maybe he'd...harmed you."

"He hasn't touched me since that day I told you everything in confessional."

"John the Brewer has been kind to you then? A better husband?"

"No," I answered. "But he's avoided me, thanks be to God."

"Thanks be to..." he said with a chuckle. His eyes glowed in the candlelight as he explained. "That afternoon during his own confession that monster once again told me of his whoring, his cruelty to his wife, and his general filth. In addition to the standard prayers, I told him he was not to touch his wife in any way for a fortnight."

"Father!" I exclaimed, my hand over my mouth. "No wonder he hasn't touched me in the last two weeks!"

We laughed far too loudly until he held up his hand to me. "Tess, seriously, it won't last. I gave you a brief reprieve from that animal. But, dear girl, the things I know..."

"My mother gave me the substance and told me to use it when he comes back from market, when his purse is full of coin."

He nodded and finished his cup of ale. "Make it without notice. If they suspect you, you'll hang. Or worse."

I nodded. I knew full well how murderous wives were treated.

"Death is worse than living with John the Brewer for one more day. The next time he raises his hand to me, it will be his last."

~

On the afternoon he returned from Lavenham, my husband stopped at the tavern. According to the account my brother gave me many years later, John the Brewer gambled, whored, and drank. The gold that made his purse heavy was gone by the time night fell.

Of course I knew none of this that fateful evening when he arrived home and dragged me by the hair from our bed to the floor.

"You want my money!" His liquor-laced breath was hot on my neck.

"No, sir," I said as calmly as I could.

"Stole my gold! You did! I saw you."

He was mad, out of his mind with thoughts of some giant conspiracy against his wealth, as small as it was. This was a recurring theme and the reason he didn't want children. To John the Brewer, a wife was little more than an indentured servant for life. Most likely, a *short* life. I was his fourth young wife, and I guessed I'd soon be his widow if I didn't act.

"Let me make you some warm ale, my husband. You are looking faint from the journey." I attempted to walk around his hulking body, but he stopped me as if I were trying to pass through a stone wall.

"So you can poison me like your mother did to your father? Evil family of witches, I should have known better. I was dazzled by your beauty, but that damn priest was right, I'll never tame you."

"Priest?"

"Don't act like you don't know he tried to get me not to marry you?"

"I had no idea, John, truly I did not. Shall I prepare some

warm water for you to clean up? I have a nice beef stew on the—"

And that's when he hit me hard across my cheekbone. With a thud, I crashed to the floor.

"My husband, I pray you not to do this. Get some rest, I'll head to the barn to sleep and tomorrow we'll—"

"You're going straight to hell," he hissed. "Tonight!"

"Is that what happened to the last ones?" I didn't care anymore – if we both died, so be it. If he did send me to hell, then I had it coming.

His eyes grew cold, evil. He raised his massive arm once more, but this time as it came down it met my knife. The blood spewed, coating the floor and me. I didn't care; it was as if I was possessed.

He moved toward me, howling in pain but intent on killing me. But this time, I had all the power. My freshly sharpened blade went through his ribs, just the way I'd seen my father butcher hogs.

More blood gushed as his massive body fell on top of mine, pinning me under him. His body shook and then stilled, his glassy eyes now stuck open for eternity.

"Burn in hell," I howled, scrambling to get out from underneath his disgusting body.

I managed to get up, but I was covered in blood.

"I have to clean up," I said out loud to the empty room. "There's so much blood…"

"Too much," he said from behind me. His voice was calm, as if this sort of thing happened every day.

I didn't answer or turn around, but simply stood there catatonic. Despite dreaming of it since the day I was betrothed, I couldn't believe what I'd just done.

"Father Gregory, how do I clean this up?"

"The blood spill is too great. Get to the church. Run, but do not take a horse. Wait for me in the crypt." He glanced around the small room as if looking for a divine answer for my sins.

My mind was empty as I walked in the darkness toward the village church. Surely I was about to be arrested, locked up, possibly tortured, and finally hanged or worse for my crime. *I should be afraid,* I thought. *But instead I feel free for the first time.*

I sat amongst the bones of the crypt below the pulpit of the stone church for hours. It was nearly dawn when the door opened and I heard his voice.

"Come, quickly," Father Gregory said.

I rose, my hands and gown coated in dried blood, and rushed to him. "Am I to be arrested?"

"No," he said. "Let's get some sleep. It's been a long night."

Confused, I followed him from the crypt. He didn't turn around until we were in a small room at the very rear of the church. "I'll bring you water to clean up. Can you start a fire?"

Is this a dream? I'm in his quarters, the man I lust after every minute of every day, and my husband is dead. Dead by my own hand! A tremor shot through my body, his eyes narrowing as he watched me.

"Stay strong, Tess. Focus on the minute by minute. Make a fire, I'll be back."

Quieting my racing mind, I focused on starting the fire in a small grate at the side of his room. Until that moment, I didn't realize he actually lived there. The room had only one small window almost at the ceiling, but once I got the fire going it was cozy and dry.

As he returned with a bucket of water, I glanced down at my bloodstained dress.

"I couldn't risk bringing anything from the house, I hope you understand."

I nodded, unable to speak.

He walked to a large trunk and brought out a simple white sleeping gown and handed it to me. "Wash, put this on, and burn that bloody dress. I'll be back soon and we'll get some sleep before they come."

They, come?

I nodded as he left the room. *So I am to be arrested*, I thought. *But at least I have a few hours with the man my soul yearns for.*

When he returned, I was sitting cross-legged on the floor in his snow white sleeping gown.

"You look angelic," he said.

"An angel about to be punished severely."

"No, Tess, that won't happen."

"I murdered a man tonight!" The numb was wearing off and the panic of fear was filling the void.

"You *murdered* no one. You *killed* a man to save your own life. Someday, in some world, that will be considered justified." He reached for the wine and poured two glasses.

"But in this world, it doesn't matter. He was my legal husband and by law could do as he wanted with me." I reached for one of the glasses, marveling at the smooth feel of it. I'd never used an actual glass before; only the cups we possessed.

He sipped his wine, deep in thought. Finally, when the glasses were empty, he spoke. "I'll sleep on the floor. Get some rest, sweet girl."

"No, I'll take the floor. Most nights he made me sleep on the ground or in the barn anyway. You've already shown me far too much kindness." I went to spread out on the hard stones, but he reached for my hand.

"There's never enough kindness for you." His hand touched mine and that familiar sensation ran through me. "Come, we'll keep each other safe and warm."

I slept that night next to him. His scent, an intoxicating

mixture of wine, vanilla, and incense drifted through my dreams. I should have had nightmares, but instead I only dreamt of him.

When I awoke the next morning, he was extinguishing the fire. He glanced over at me with a troubled smile.

"You look worried," I said, rubbing the sleep out of my eyes.

"Let me worry for both of us."

"Are they coming for me?"

"No, of course not." He poked away the last of the embers of our fire.

"Can I talk to my mother?"

He shook his head.

"Father Gregory, when can I see her then?"

A cloud of sadness floated over his face. "Call me Edmond. We're beyond the Father thing forever. When we are alone, please always use my given name."

"Edmond, when can I see my mother?"

His lips formed a tense line before he said, "Never."

"How long will I stay here? In the church? Have you taken me into sanctuary?"

"Not exactly. That only works for the nobility. No, commoners, and lately even kings, just get dragged out into the light and slaughtered."

"Then what will I do?"

"We'll leave after the funeral."

"I can't go to *his* funeral!"

A dark smile wiped away his sadness. "Not John the Brewer's, dear Tess. *Yours.*"

EDMOND

"What's to become of me then?" Tess asked.

I sat across from her, taking her hands in mine. As I touched her again, I knew I was about to fall off the very edge of the universe. The night prior, we shared a bed and it took every ounce of self-control I had not to touch her. My Tess, in my bed, our bodies touching; it was heaven.

"In the eyes of everyone you have ever known, you died last night. Your husband came home, drunker than they've ever seen him by all accounts, and set the house on fire. There was a poker found, and some other objects, but you were both burned to a crisp."

"And his heir?" My husband's business was still worth money, and he owned the land our house and brewery sat on outright.

"Your mother. He had no one other than you."

"But wouldn't my father inherit then?"

"He's gone, too. Passed away due to a severe stomach ailment, they say." I shot her a wink as the knowing look drifted across her face. "My condolences."

"That donkey had it coming! I just can't believe she finally did it."

"Your mother is in a far better financial standing now, it seems. Of course she's lost her husband *and* her daughter in one night."

"Can you tell her? Please?"

"I think she suspects, but I can't risk it just now. Once you are safe, possibly then."

"I have nothing," she said, looking down at the sleeping gown I loaned her. "What will I do? Can I be your servant, Father?"

"Edmond," I corrected. "And no, you'll never serve me. I think, though, you may be destined to serve God."

The color drained from her usually rosy cheeks. "I couldn't…"

"We'll talk later. I have a glorious funeral ceremony to prepare, paid for by your newly-moneyed mother."

"Is there also to be a funeral for…for him?"

"No," I answered with a broad smile. "It seems no one cares that John the Brewer has been sent straight to hell."

~

That afternoon I sent two trusted riders out, a gold coin to each assuring their loyalty. Two sealed messages, from my very own ring, went off to my sister at Stoneham Abbey and to my uncle, Bishop Gregory, in Cambridge. One of them was sure to have a solution to my problem.

After the funeral for her daughter, Tess' mother requested that I hear her confession. The second my door closed, she spoke. "Forgive me Father, for I have sinned."

"I'm not sure I'm the one to hear this confession, Eleanor."

Her dressed rustled from the other side of the booth. "You are exactly the one to hear it, Father Gregory."

"Proceed then, but keep your voice quite low."

"Is she well? Tell me that first."

"She is," I answered against my better judgment.

I heard her exhale. "Tell her that I love her, always, and that she did the right thing."

"This topic is dangerous, dear lady. What sins do you feel the need to unburden yourself of?"

"I poisoned my husband and encouraged my daughter to rid herself of her own wicked husband."

"Are you sorry for these sins?"

"No." She laughed, the joy of freedom ringing throughout the small wooden booth. "I thank God every day to be rid of those demons."

"As do I." I leaned forward so she could see my face, my finger across my lips. "No one must know. No one!"

"Yes, Father."

That night, I decided it was time for us to ride to Cambridge under the cover of darkness. I couldn't risk waiting for help from my family; keeping Tess near town was far too dangerous. I left a sprawled note about a family emergency in London as we headed in the other direction on my horse.

At dawn, we hid in an abandoned barn. To get her proper clothes would have risked someone noticing, so she remained dressed in my clothes, and that was sure to stand out. I needed time to prepare before we rode into the city.

It was hot that day in the barn, so we lounged in the loft eating apples and dried meat from my saddlebag. When I brought out a flask of wine, she giggled like a little girl. She was beautiful.

"You have so much wine! The church is that rich?"

"Well, yes," I answered. "In general, sinfully so. But as far as the parish, not so much. I come from a wealthy family – we are major landowners in Norfolk. My brother is—"

"The Earl of Norwich!"

I nodded.

"Oh my!" she said. "That is a big name. Gregory! *Lord* Gregory! I remember my father saying that once on that first Sunday."

"That's my brother now, but was my father before him," I said. "But me, I was the second son. Of course when my father died all the land and the title that went with it was bestowed on my brother. Like many second sons from wealthy families, I was sent to seminary and made to join the church."

"And your uncle, Bishop Gregory?"

"Also a second son after my father."

"I guess I thought wealth, power, and all that comes with it made one free."

I pulled closer to her. "No, it just hangs different nooses around your neck."

TESS

Next to me in the straw, Edmond's hand drifted to my leg and slowly grew nearer and nearer to the very heart of my body. It drew near to a place that I feared was scarred forever from the harsh treatment by John the Brewer.

"I desire you, more than any man, but my knowledge of physical love is *most* unpleasant." My hand grasped his, the familiar spark of energy passing between us.

"That was not love, dear Tess, that was cruelty."

"It is all I have ever known. Indeed, it is all I have ever seen."

"Your father was not a good man," Edmond said. "But have you never seen actual love? Affection from a man to a woman, or otherwise?"

I thought back to my younger years. "My grandparents, I suppose. My mother's father is the one who taught me to read. He was a good man, and treated my grandmother as if she were a precious treasure to be honored."

"That is how it should be."

"Have you been in love, Edmond?"

"Twice," he said with a warm smile.

"Oh please tell me."

"Well, when I was young I lived in a beautiful palace with my older sister, Joan. We studied alongside the royal blood of England. And we also played alongside them."

"And?" I said, as intrigued as when I heard fairy tales as a child.

"And one afternoon while I was out hunting, one of my royal companions kissed me. It was a kiss so perfect, I've never, in all of my dalliances, experienced such a thing since."

"A kiss…" I mused. "I've never been kissed."

He was astounded. "Tess Darby! That is a tragedy."

"Perhaps, a wonderful man might come along and rectify such a travesty?" I leaned in close to him, my face turned up to his, praying that he would kiss me.

But he pulled away. "One does not rush the sort of thing you desire."

"No?"

"No, my darling. You are a miracle from our creator, one to be savored."

"Savored," I repeated, the heat rising to my breast.

"Unwrapped slowly, like the finest gift."

I took a deep breath as his fingers reached to cradle my chin. His eyes met mine, and when he had my full attention, he said, "You are beautiful, and we will go slowly. But I *will* have you, Tess Darby."

I nodded, unable to form words.

The very tip of his nose met mine, and he held the gaze until I could bear no more. My eyelids fluttered closed like a butterfly's wings.

"So perfect," he groaned, his lips nearing mine but not yet touching.

I wanted him as I'd never wanted anything before. There

was nothing Edmond would be denied that afternoon in the barn.

He breathed deeply, the warmth of his exhale turning me fluid.

Finally, after what seemed like forever, his lips met my own, but there was no kiss...not yet. He simply held his lips to mine and waited.

But I could wait no more. I crushed my lips to his, intoxicated by him. His lips parted, but still he hesitated. My Edmond waited, waited until in a frenzy of need, my own mouth opened to him. We became one in that moment, more so than during any other touch I'd ever experienced.

I never wanted it to end, but when his lips finally left mine, we both knew everything had changed.

"So *that* is what all the fuss is about!" I said with a deep sigh.

He drew me close so that my head rested on his chest.

"But you must tell me about the *second* time you were in love," I said.

"Hm?"

"You said you'd been in love twice."

"Ah, yes." His fingers wrapped around a lock of my hair as I listened to his heartbeat. "Well Tess, the first time was with the royal kisser I mentioned. And the second time..."

"Oh please tell me!"

"The second time I hope will last forever."

My heart pounded against my ribcage and my palms grew clammy. *He was still in love with her! With someone else!*

"The second time of course is with your fine self."

"Me!"

He chuckled a little, his chest rising and falling as I clung to him. "I love you."

"And I you!" I said far too loudly. *He loves me!*

"And, my beautiful girl, *that* kiss put all others to shame."

~

We left the safety of the barn at dusk. Wearing only the thin sleeping gown he'd given me, I shivered in the night air.

"Are you cold, dear girl?"

I nodded, wrapping my arm around my chest. "A little. I'll be fine."

He reached into his bag and pulled out the heavy priestly robe. Since we left Worthington, he'd only worn regular clothes.

"It's warm, and I have a blanket also."

I giggled. "Isn't it blasphemy for me to wear clerical garments?"

He smiled wide and winked. "I can't think of anyone more holy than you, my love."

"I'm warmer just hearing you call me that."

"You *are* my love." He kissed me again, and I felt as if I could fly. "And besides," he said, putting the heavy robe over my head. "Soon you will be wearing your own holy apparel."

"What?" I asked, my head popping through the neck of the tunic.

"Tess Darby is dead. She died with her husband, the brewer, in a horrible fire. Currently, I'm escorting my cousin, *Sister* Elizabeth Gregory, to her new assignment at the great abbey near Cambridge."

"I can't! Oh Edmond, I *cannot* do what you ask of me."

"You must, my sweet one. It's the only way I can think of to keep you hidden."

"But…"

His eyebrow rose quizzically.

"But," I said, my voice lowering to barely a whisper. "I'm no longer a maid."

He laughed a loud belly laugh. "Half the nuns in that damnable place aren't virgins! Most are still fornicating openly with whomever they are able to. Oh, Tess, I mean *Elizabeth*, the things you are about to learn about this world!"

~

At nightfall, we left the warmth of the barn and headed toward Cambridge. Unfortunately, the weather did not cooperate.

"We cannot ride in this rain!" Edmond yelled back to me. The wind howled, and the rain was coming at us sideways.

Edmond left the road, guiding his horse toward a heavy stand of trees. "Here, under this overhang!"

Under the shelter of the heavy boughs, we dismounted our horse. "That was miserable," he said. "I'm soaked through."

I looked down at the heavy wool robe I wore. "I'm dry underneath."

He managed a small smile. "At least those dreaded rags are good for something."

The wool priest's robe was far too big for me, and even my bare feet were protected from the elements under its hefty weight.

"I'm going for firewood. We'll need to wait this deluge out." He turned to walk deeper into the forest.

"Please be careful," I called out after him.

"Always, my love, always."

When he was out of sight, I tied up the horse and looked through the leather saddlebag. "Hm, what can we cook up?" I said to myself.

At that moment, I was grabbed from behind.

"Look, Louis, a priest!"

I fought against the man, but to no avail.

Another man came out of the cover of the brush, and

then another followed. There were three of them, and the one who held me seemed immovable.

"A pretty priest?" Louis asked, walking around to the front of me. "I wouldn't mind a little bit of..." He paused, staring into my hooded face. Laughing, he yanked the hood back. "It's a girl, Pierre!"

The man he called Pierre tossed me to the ground. "Tonight is going to be fun, boys! But I'm first."

He yanked his breeches down, his half wilted member barely protruding from the mass of dark hair that encircled it.

"Don't," I said, my voice dead calm.

"Be good and we might let you live," the stinking man hissed as he fell onto me.

"Final warning."

The men laughed, as if my threats were meaningless. "A brave one, Claude!" Pierre looked over to the third man, still partially hidden in the heavy brush. He was holding something with a rope, something I could not see.

Louis came close, hovering behind Pierre. "Hurry up, I'm next," he said.

When Pierre pulled up the heavy tunic, however, his mistake turned deadly. My blade sliced through his side, and before he even knew what happened, I'd stuck the cold metal into his heart.

It happened so fast that Louis barely had time to react. "Claude, bring the dog!" he screamed, but it was too late for him. My agile knife was already lodged in his left eye, followed by his right, and ultimately, straight into his gut.

I leapt to my feet, pulling the knife from the oozing innards of Louis.

"Don't come near me!"

"A few lucky jabs to two stupid, careless men doesn't

make you any match for me, bitch." Claude walked toward me, yanking the rope he held.

Behind him was a massive, snarling black bundle of fur.

"Edmond!" I screamed, my voice echoing throughout the rainy night.

"Let's get this done before *Edmond* gets back, little girl."

"Edmond!" I screamed again.

"Relax, stupid woman. You're not my type. Besides, you did me a favor. Now I don't have to share whatever's in that saddlebag three ways. Toss it over here and I'll be on my way."

"No." I held the knife out in front of me.

He yanked the rope, but before the dog reached me, I threw the knife at the man's head, lodging it directly in his face. He fell to the ground.

As he fell, the dog leapt toward me, pinning me down. The thing snarled, growled, but did not bite me. As my left hand rose up, my second knife ready to strike the animal, a voice stopped me.

"No, don't!"

"Edmond, please help! This beast is going to kill me."

"Stay your blade, my love."

He walked toward us, his hand out to the snarling dog. "There, there. Come," he said, backing away. The dog followed. After a few deep breaths, I realized the dog was off of me and I was unharmed.

"Kill it! Get rid of that beast," I begged.

"He's no beast, he's just a little puppy. Aren't you, boy?" He knelt dog in front of the dog, and within minutes the thing was licking his very hand.

"See? He's a good boy. It was just a little misunderstanding with our dear Tess, wasn't it, boy?" The dog nuzzled into Edmond as if they'd grown up together.

"How did you do that?" I brushed myself off, surveying the three dead men I'd left in my wake.

"I have my talents too, my darling. Less bloody than yours most definitely."

I nodded, reaching my own hand out to the dog who attacked me minutes earlier. He licked my hand and panted.

"What should we call him?" Edmond asked.

"Beast!"

He laughed. "Yes, Beast. It's perfect, seriously!"

~

We slept under the heavy robes, our new friend Beast refusing to rest. Instead, like a sentry, he paced our perimeter. "What's he doing?" I asked Edmond.

"He's guarding us."

"Surely he needs to sleep?"

Edmond yawned and said, "He can rest tomorrow. We'll need to wait until the cover of darkness to ride toward Cambridge anyhow."

"Well, I do feel safer," I admitted.

"It's his calling, what he does. He protects the good. That's why he would not attack you as the men wished. If you had not dispatched them, Beast would have."

"How do you know?" I was sure he was teasing me.

Edmond yawned again, rolling over into sleep. "Because he told me."

We slept soundly, wrapped in each other's arms. We rose at dawn the next morning, hungry but warm and dry.

Edmond squinted his eyes toward the lush green valley. "Should I get us some fresh meat?"

"I sense that I'm more likely the one to get my hands bloody for this cause, your holy father."

He jabbed a finger playfully into my ribs. "I grew up hunting, Tess. I hunted with royals, after all. You, my love, shall have fresh venison for your morning meal."

"Venison is a bit lofty for now, my lord," I teased.

He shook his head. "C'mon Tess, we've seen tons of deer on our ride. I'll be back momentarily with the biggest stag you've ever seen."

I smiled at him. "Well, my mighty huntsman, I guess I'd better gather more firewood in the meantime."

"Yes, that would be most helpful. Try not to get into too much trouble before I return?"

I leaned up and kissed him before he walked off into the brush.

"Deer," I laughed after he'd gone. My Edmond had taken none of the weapons needed to actually hunt a deer successfully. I had, however, spied plenty of fresh meat right there around our campsite.

He returned hours later, dirty and empty-handed. "They were too fast! If only I had my bow..." he grumbled.

"No worries, my love. Sit by the fire. I'll have the meat roasting soon enough."

He looked puzzled as he pulled off his muddy boots. "Meat?"

I tilted my head toward the large rock I'd been using to skin the rabbits. "Well, not venison, but rabbit stew will do nicely. I even found wild onions and some herbs growing by the stream."

He rubbed his temples and smiled. "I'm afraid, dear resourceful Tess, that you are stuck with a useless cleric."

"Oh, I have lots of uses for you, Father Gregory." I winked at him. "But first, let's eat."

We ate the rabbit stew steaming hot from the pot he'd brought. Afterward, we opened our last bottle of French wine, sharing it directly from the bottle. "Where did you learn to do all that?" he asked.

"From starving, Edmond. Hunger and need are a powerful motivation to learn to provide."

He nodded. "I've never been without, I suppose. Hunting for us was sport rather than about the need to eat."

"Early on I found I was quick. Even as a young child, I could sneak in places undetected. My father used to call me a specter, and he sure didn't mean it as a compliment. Hunting rabbits is a matter of speed and stillness."

"And we all know you're good with a knife."

I nodded. "Yes, it was just natural for me. I can make this blade do whatever I wish, it seems. I've seen men struggle to skin rabbits, but I just seem to have a feel for using that blade deftly."

"Rabbits, wicked highwaymen, monstrous husbands…"

"Especially monstrous husbands! But all of it brought me to you."

"You are like no woman I've ever known."

"Because I'm an original!" I boasted childishly. But my Edmond didn't mind, he merely took me into his arms and kissed me again.

～

That afternoon, with his belly full and the day warm, Edmond fell sound asleep by the fire. Confident that Beast was there to guard over him, I decided to explore a nearby manor house we'd passed.

In the gentle breeze, the lady of the house's fine laundry was drying in the sun. From the cover of the shrubbery, I eyed my choices. The sensible choice would have been the plain frock on the very edge of the line, but a ruby silk gown covered in delicate golden needlework caught my eye.

I'd never seen a garment so beautiful, and I moved to take it. And I could have; I could have been in and out of the courtyard as fast as lightning. But I heard a noise that gave me pause. A woman was screaming from the kitchen, a small brick building at the side of the great manor house.

"Hurry! We don't have time to save the baby," the voice said.

"No! You will not kill it," another voice begged.

I sat the precious dress on the ground and peered through the opened window. "Jayne, you'll both die. If the master finds out you bore his child, he will kill you both anyway."

"He'll never find out. My brother is waiting."

"Your brother is waiting for a live child," the older woman said. "The cord is wrapped around his neck; he isn't breathing. We must cut the whole mess loose and destroy it before we are found out."

"No!" the one called Jayne wailed.

I looked at the bundle in her arms. The cord was wrapped around the infant's neck, so tightly that the child was blue.

Before I could stop myself, I stood before the two women. Their mouths fell open as I spoke. "He's not dead."

The older one stared at me, her face as pale as if she'd seen a ghost. She fell to her knees and chanted some prayer.

"Help me, please!" Jayne begged.

I reached for my most delicate blade and rushed toward the suffocating baby boy. "I've seen this in sheep countless times. The trick is to free the baby lamb from the cord without damage to the neck."

Ignoring the sobs of the women, all of my focus went into the delicate cutting. I was fully aware that one wrong slice and the child would be dead. Even worse, it had to be done quickly.

Focus, Tess! I scolded myself, steadying my hand for the final portion of cord. Within seconds, the baby cried. His mother clasped him to her chest, and as he turned pink, they both began to pray.

But they were praying to *me*!

"Oh no my ladies, I am no…"

"Angel, you are an angel sent by God to save my child from death!"

My eyes widened. I looked down at Edmond's long white sleeping gown, now bloody from the surgery. My bare feet poked out underneath, and my hair was flowing over my shoulders. Since I was practically naked anyway, I hadn't bothered to put it up. To them, I was a sign from God himself. To me, I was a thief there to rob them.

"I came only to borrow a dress, I heard the cries. I've birthed so many lambs that I couldn't help but—"

"You are an angel," a voice said from behind me. "Praise be to God."

"My lady!" Both women bowed as the baby nuzzled to his mother's breast.

I turned to see a tall dark haired woman dressed in an emerald green velvet gown. She bowed to *me*. "You have chosen to save this child, and we will serve you."

I shook my head. "I am simply a peasant thief, I needed a dress, nothing more."

She smiled at me and looked to her two kitchen servants. "Today we have entertained angels, and we have been truly blessed. This is a sign from on high."

"A sign?" the older servant asked.

"A sign that my husband's young plaything here shall leave us. Take your child and go," she said to Jayne.

"Yes my lady, thank you, my lady!"

I was completely unaware of what to do, but I knew I needed to get out of there.

"Yes, my children," I said stupidly. "I have been sent here to take these two souls to safety."

Jayne rose quickly, nearly slipping on the afterbirth that

coated the floor beneath her. I steadied her as we left the kitchen behind.

The baby nuzzled into her arms, breathing as if nothing had ever threatened to harm him. "The dress," Jayne said. She pointed to the ground in front of the window. "Get the dress."

"You know I'm not really an angel."

"You are our angel. You've saved us both today. My brother was going to hide the baby until I could escape, but now we are both free and I can start a new life with my child. So please, take the dress and whatever else you wish."

I picked up the dress, and as she ran with the child toward a young man waiting by the gate, she shouted back to me. "And there are embroidered slippers over on the bench, get those too!"

"God bless you!" I answered.

"He just did. I'll never forget you, my guardian angel in white."

The bloody gown discarded, I walked back to camp wrapped in my new finery. As I turned the corner, I saw Edmond roasting our three remaining rabbits over a fire. Beast ran toward me, sniffing at the new dress.

"Out shopping, were we?" he teased.

"I saw a manor house about a mile back. I might have been tempted..."

"How many men did you kill?"

"None!"

"Well that's a first."

"Look Edmond, I even have shoes!"

He rotated the rabbits on their spits. "It does seem a pity to cover such perfect feet, but they are lovely."

"I think this is pure silk! I've never owned a dress so fine." I couldn't stop touching it.

"You look beautiful, Bess."

"I've only ever had two dresses at a time. One to work in, and one for Sundays. I feel like a queen!"

"You are *my* queen."

After pulling the rabbits off the fire, he took me into his arms. "My beautiful Bess. But now I'm starving. Let's eat."

"I need to wash my hands first. They're bloody."

He took a deep breath and lifted my right hand to his face. "I thought you said no lives were lost this fine day?"

"No, not this time. But I did have to assist with a childbirth."

He shook his head and grinned. "As one does in their silk dress before lunch."

~

I'd hoped for one more night in the countryside by a fire with Edmond. After our kiss in the barn loft, we'd engaged in many forms of touching and I was always bathed in endless kisses. He had not, however, again moved to fully consummate our union. But I was ready, and I intended to have him. Right then, right there.

Except, I lost my nerve. "Let's pack up camp, Tess," he said, oblivious to my scheme to bed him, once and for all.

"Pack up? Er, I thought we couldn't move until after dark?"

"You are well disguised now, my lady. Besides, I'm tiring of adventures. I need a bed, a decent meal, and gallons of good wine."

I tried not to pout. "You're right. But this gown is so heavy – how do I ride in it?"

"I'll show you, my beloved. It's not the most efficient way to travel, but I think we'll be able to get into Cambridge without too many stares."

Hours later, with our constant companion trotting alongside us, we rode into the largest city I'd ever seen. From behind him, I marveled, "It's bigger than Lavenham!"

He laughed. "Lavenham is tiny! My love, you are about to see so many things."

"With you, I hope." I nuzzled into his back. With Edmond in regular clothes and me in my new gown, we looked like any other members of the landed gentry.

"Always with me. Listen Tess, my sister, Joan, is meeting us at the tavern," he said. "She's secured rooms for us for a few nights while you train."

"*Rooms*? Plural?"

He squeezed my hand. "To look proper, my darling. But the rooms are connected."

I smiled. I couldn't bear the thought of not falling asleep on his chest, my fingers wrapped in his silky curls. And besides, I was determined to become fully his as soon as possible.

"You said while I train. Train for what?" I asked as we neared the bustling tavern.

"To be a nun."

I stopped in the dusty street like a stubborn mule. "I will not!"

He pulled my hand. "I told you it's the only way. Come, my darling, it's far too dangerous for us to tarry in public. Even in this gown, you could be recognized."

PART II
CAMBRIDGE, EAST ANGLIA,
ENGLAND

EDMOND

"*E*dmond!" she screamed like a child at the village faire.

"Sis!" I howled back, equally as excited. I hadn't seen my sister Joan in nearly a year, and I'd missed her dearly.

"I mean *Sister* Joan," I corrected with a wide smile. "Or is it Mother Gregory?"

She smacked me playfully. "And who ever thought that my devious little brother would ever be Father Gregory?"

I shook my head, taking her into my arms. "You know the choice, unlike yours, was not my own."

She rested her head on my shoulder, her long headpiece cascading over my back. "It's not such a terrible life is it? Serving God?"

I let out a deep breath. We'd never agree on matters of religion. "You know how I feel about that."

She nodded, her head still resting on me. "I do. What about serving your community then? The peasants who rely on the facets of the church to give reason to their dull, too-short lives?"

My sister was always an idealist. "True. And I do love the

teaching part. It's just…I'm not free. I'm trapped in a role that I had no say in, and I will be for life."

"We're all trapped, none of us are free on this earth. Make the best of it, Edmond. Maybe when Uncle is pope…"

I laughed loudly enough to shake her lovely head off my shoulder. "Sis, that is never going to happen."

"He said it would. If that happens, we'll live like kings!"

"I've seen the dark side of kings, no thank you."

She sighed, her green eyes locking onto mine. "Find joy where you can. That's the only way to truly be free."

"Speaking of joy," I said, glancing back toward my disguised beloved at the tavern entrance.

"This is dangerous, my brother." She leveled her eyes at me. "Are you sure you want to do this? For a peasant?"

I understood her trepidation, but I also knew that there was no going back now. I was in far too deep. And, for the first time I could remember, happy.

~

That afternoon in small set of rooms atop the bustling tavern, Tess Darby was no more. In her place was Sister Elizabeth Gregory.

"If all the sisters looked like that, I might not mind the priesthood!" I said.

"Now, now, Father Gregory," Joan scolded.

With a deep breath, my love walked to me. I could see the fear in her eyes.

"You can do this, Tess. Trust me."

Joan spoke up. "Never use that name again, Edmond. Everyone is listening. The abbey is so devoid of entertainment that gossip is the most popular pastime. And, I assure you, all eyes will be on you. *And* her."

"I'll try to use Bess instead. Tess, Bess — easy switch."

The newly-named Sister Elizabeth looked up at me. "I'm not taking holy orders? You promised!"

I shook my head. "No, of course not. We simply need to hide you for a while."

"Please don't leave me." Her voice shook, breaking my heart. I wasn't used to my girl being afraid.

She pressed against me, the rough feel of the nun's habit she wore so different than her normal clothes.

"Edmond can stay for a season," Joan said. "I am the abbess, and he is my brother. The sisters will be so thrilled to have a handsome man around, they won't pay much attention to a new sister."

"Of course they won't," I agreed. "And we are all family, so naturally we shall be quite close, won't we my dear cousin Elizabeth?"

"So close," she said. I longed to take her into my arms and hold her close.

Joan rose to leave. "I'll send for you in the morning. I need to prepare your rooms."

"Keep them near to each other," I said with a wink.

"You keep my secrets and I'll endeavor to keep yours," Joan said from the doorway.

"You have secrets, older sister?"

"You'll find out soon enough, unfortunately."

～

After Joan left us, I reached for Elizabeth. Beast was curled up in the corner, content to be gnawing on a bone the tavern keeper had given him.

Elizabeth looked worried. "I can't do this. I've barely ever even been around nuns!"

"No one expects you to actually *do* anything, Tess. I mean…Bess."

"I'll never get used to that!"

"You are alive, and we are together," I said.

She nodded, leading me toward the small bed in the corner. "I've loved you since that first day," she said. Her hands caressed down my chest, pulling at my shirt.

"I love you so much."

Her hands went lower. "Edmond, what if this is our last night to be fully alone?" I wanted her more than I wanted air. And, I was unsure how much privacy we'd get in the convent. Or, for that matter, how long I'd be allowed to stay.

She paused as we undressed, a look of worry drifting across her eyes. "What is it, my darling? Do we need to let the scars of the past heal first?"

"You have healed me, my love. It's just…"

"Just?" I asked.

"I desire you so much, Edmond. But you took vows, you were my priest."

"Damn the vows, damn it all. I need you now, Bess."

SISTER ELIZABETH GREGORY

"*Y*ou are my church; *you* are my religion."

The words came from his perfect lips as pure as any prayer ever uttered. My Edmond, my love – I couldn't bear to look into his eyes. Despite the swell of lust in my very core, I *should* not lie with my priest. And yet... the fire of our love was far more powerful than any threat of hell fire. The force between us was far too strong, and would swallow us both alive.

"But you took holy vows," my lips said once again in a forced protest.

He drew closer, the warmth of his breath on my neck. "*You* are holy; *love* is holy. How could anything *this* perfect ever be loathsome in the eyes of He who created you?"

His kisses enveloped me until the fire deep in me exploded like a log in the flames. Pulling me close, his warm lips glided across my neck. This man was all I'd thought of, all I'd dreamed of since the night he'd brought me to safety.

"We mustn't..." I whimpered in a half-hearted protest. "What if it's wrong?"

"It could never be anything but right, my darling girl." His lips went higher, skating across my skin and finding my lips. When his warm tongue found mine, I knew there would never be another for me. If I couldn't have him, then I would play my role willingly. Without him, a life of celibacy would be my life sentence.

He pulled me closer, the hardness under his leather trousers grinding against my torso, causing the heat to rise within me as if I had the sweating sickness. My body was an inferno at the slightest touch from him.

"Please," was all I could manage to say. "Please," I begged again.

"Please *what*, Sister Elizabeth?" His breath was hot on my lips, his body pressed into mine.

"Please take me, Father Gregory. Quickly, now, or I will die."

"Slowly," he breathed. "I shall go slowly. Only after you're screaming in pleasure, only then will I give in to the lust burning deep within me."

"Slowly," I repeated as he stripped me of my new tunic. "I've never known slowly. Only rough, and painful."

He took my face in his hands, and his eyes enveloped me. "Never will you be hurt again."

"Is this what love is?"

"It's what our love is." As our lips pressed together, the heat between us took over. Fear evaporated as our bodies merged into one.

"Only when you're ready," he said. His fingers ran across my belly, down to the place where no man had ever touched so gently. Softly, he caressed me until I shook with a sensation I'd never know. It was as if my soul left my body. And, when it stopped, he entered me and it started all over again.

"I can take more!" But as he thrust, it happened yet again. "Edmond, I'm going to burst!"

He slowed his stroke, his tongue finding my own once

again. As we kissed, I felt him quicken. My legs grasped him as he shook, and in an explosion of energy, my teeth sank into his neck.

When he collapsed on top of me, I knew an entire new world had opened before me.

"Oh Bess, you are magic!"

I nuzzled into him in the moonlight. "I never understood why some chose to mate."

"To mate!" he laughed.

"It seemed thus to me. There was never tenderness, never such pleasure!"

"My darling, I shall bring you boundless pleasure every chance that I get."

We fell fast asleep wrapped in one another. At dawn, I woke him up to have him again.

"So eager!" he teased.

"Is that a bad thing?" I had no experience with a relationship, with love.

"Oh no," he growled, his teeth landing at the back of my neck as he sank deep inside me.

~

The next morning, a thin young nun arrived at the tavern.

"I'm here from the abbey, Edmond, I am Ursula." She spoke only to him, ignoring me as if I were invisible. He stared at her, genuinely astounded. Even I understood that the world of the clergy was formal, with a cut-in-stone hierarchy and protocol.

"Most sisters refer to me as Father Gregory," he corrected sternly.

"And most Fathers aren't sneaking around with nuns in taverns!" she said, glaring at me as if I had the plague.

"I see," he said simply. "Shall we go then?"

"Yes, *Edmond*, Joan is waiting for us."

I looked over to Beast, gesturing for him to come.

"Oh, you must leave that mongrel here."

I felt tears well up, but out of pure stubbornness, refused to cry. I would be strong for Edmond and even stronger for me. I'd survived so much; I could survive this. "I think the innkeeper will care for him, Edmond. He's been feeding him better than he feeds us."

Edmond shook his head and brought Beast by his side. Inches from the dour Sister Ursula's face, he spoke. "You'll show the necessary respect, or I'll have you scrubbing my floors. Our dog will stay by our side, and that is final."

She made a face, but didn't dare argue with him.

～

It was a short ride to the abbey, and Beast followed along like a loyal friend.

True to her word, his sister Joan put our rooms next to each other in a wing that was empty – at least we'd have privacy.

That night after dinner and services, he slipped into my room. I fell into him, relieved. Once in his arms, my fingers wrapped around a ringlet of his dark curls. My Edmond. Perfect. Eternal. Holy.

"Darling Elizabeth," he said. "There is none other before you."

My heartbeat quickened, my breath was shallow. There was nothing other than him.

His wry smile wrapped around his face. "If I cannot taste you, I will die."

"Die?" I asked. "So dramatic!"

He dropped to his knees before me, his heavy robes brushing the rustic floor.

"Sister, may I?" He lifted the stiff fabric of my skirts.

"I-I've never, what are you doing?" Never had a man been on his knees before me, attempting to do the thing he was suggesting.

"I told you that I must taste you. *All* of you." His fingers skated up the skin of my bare legs. When his face dipped under the cloth of my nightgown, my knees buckled.

"Father!" I moaned.

"So sweet," he murmured against the skin of my thighs. "So very sweet."

Edmond's eager tongue lapped at me, toward my sex, toward the very fire that burned from my loins. I could take no more when he entered me, licking, kissing sucking, nearly begging with his lips. "God, Bess," he moaned, inhaling me with desire.

The very essence of me melted away as he took me using only his mouth, in a way I'd never known. It was if he worshiped me; the very heart of me.

When his tongue would not stop, and I could not cease quaking, I begged, "Edmond! Stop. I can take no more. I must now have you in this way. I want you fully."

The heavy robe he wore fell to the floor. In perfect glory, before me, my Edmond was naked. "Your Grace," I said, falling to my knees.

I took him into my mouth, beyond my lips, down my very throat.

"Bess!" he groaned as I took him deep, swallowing to fight the natural choke-reflex. I wanted more of him; all of him.

EDMOND

"*Y*our angel of death is quite skilled, it would seem," my uncle said one afternoon. Merely days after we'd settled in to the abbey, he'd called for me. I wasn't surprised. He was up to something, but then again, he was always up to something.

"It would seem she has a strong instinct for survival." I tried to sound as if I didn't care, as if Bess were any other peasant-turned-nun. We all knew she wasn't, however.

He sighed deeply and leaned back in his favorite velvet chair. "I have use of her talents."

My head snapped up. "Don't touch her! She is mine." No one touched my Elizabeth.

"Settle down," he said with a chuckle, his palm raised toward me. "Not for *that*. Heaven knows I have plenty of *that*."

"What do you want of her?" I was still angry.

"Errant priest over in Ipswich that I need taken care of."

"Taken care of?"

He winked at me and nodded.

"Sister Elizabeth needs to stay hidden; hidden and innocent. Besides, I won't have her put in harm's way."

"Innocent," he laughed. "How many has she silently butchered?"

"One! And she had no choice."

"One that you know of. And it was a *good* choice. Relax my boy, I'm on your side."

One, and then some highwaymen, and who knows who else, I thought. "Get her out of England. Let us do work there, but here it is far too dangerous."

"If she's as good as I think she is, she'll be in and out undetected. Edmond, her stay comes at a price. Your…nearness, shall we say, also comes at a price."

"Why? What is so important that she needs to dirty her hands over?"

"It has come to my attention that Father Rybalt is taking liberties with his altar boys. Unfathomable, unholy liberties."

My mind was racing. I certainly couldn't abide lecherous clergy, especially went it came to innocent boys, but my Elizabeth wasn't the answer.

"No," I said. And no one *ever* told him no.

He merely flashed me an evil, cold smile. "She's already on her way to Ipswich. Sister Elizabeth shared none of your concerns for her safety or her *innocence.* Now, prepare for dinner. Your brother is here to dine with us."

∼

I wanted to go to Bess, but I knew I had to appease my uncle first. So, despite the howling in my brain, I acted as if all was well as I walked into the banquet room.

My older brother was sitting at the long mahogany table. Based on the glassiness of his eyes, I guessed he was already a few glasses of wine in.

"Jerome," I said with a polite nod.

"Ah dear younger brother, there you are. Tell me, is it comfortable wearing dresses all day?"

I shrugged, used to his incessant teasing. "Tell me, older brother, is it tiresome acting like a fool all day?"

He raised his glass to me. "To men in dresses."

I poured my own glass and raised it to him. "To useless fools."

He laughed and shook his head. "So I heard this odd rumor today. Perhaps you can illuminate it for me."

"Such a big word, brother. Have you been studying?"

His fingers formed an offensive gesture as he drained his glass. "Apparently our cousin Elizabeth is back from the dead."

I gulped hard, willing myself to show no emotion. "Perhaps you should take this up with the mighty bishop."

"Oh I did, and received the usual scolding. He hates me, you know."

"Yes." My uncle wasn't at all fond of Jerome, but he'd been my father's favorite. That was probably *why* my uncle hated him.

"Do *you* hate me, Edmond?"

I sighed and drained my glass. My brother was a pain in my backside, but he wasn't evil. Not completely evil, anyway. Just annoying. "Hate is a strong word."

"Who is she? The girl?"

I waved my hand in the air, as if the topic were irrelevant. "Oh, honestly Jerome, it's nothing. The whole thing is quite embarrassing, if you must know."

"Oh, brother, I must know. And embarrassing makes it even more intriguing. Besides, I have a right to know because I've been asked to restore her allowance."

"By whom?" I said, far more loudly than I should have.

"Her father."

"Her murderer."

"It was a suicide."

I stared at him until he shrugged. "Either way, it's costing our family money. He's demanded that I pay for his silence."

"Then you must," I said. "Otherwise Uncle will get involved, and I assure you it won't end well for either of you."

"Was that a threat, dear brother?"

"It was advice. This issue is far more than you want to get involved in."

He refilled our glasses as the dinner bell rang in the grand hallway. "I'll play along. But, who is she? At least, what's the story you're going to feed me?"

"I may have become involved with a local girl in Worthington."

"I always knew you were never cut out for the cloth. So you couldn't keep it in your pants, er, your dress."

"Robe," I corrected.

He laughed, loving any opportunity to ridicule me. I'd always been popular with women, *and* men, but Jerome was awkward and couldn't seem to find a match. I could count on one hand the number of times he'd bedded someone, and that included the ones he'd paid for.

"I'll pay Uncle Idiot to leave it alone. But do me a favor, let Uncle Reginald know I'm doing you a favor?"

"Of course. And thank you."

"So the rest? Why try to pass some girl you laid with as cousin Elizabeth?"

"It was the only way to keep her."

His eyes went wide, and then he laughed. And laughed. And finally, he pointed his shaking index finger at me. "No way! Father Edmond Gregory, the handsome, the Casanova, the lover of the century, is in love? This is the best thing I've heard…ever!"

I cringed at him. "I'm just a man. But yes, she did possibly make an imprint on my heart. They were going to betroth her to another, someone unthinkable, so we…extracted her."

He slapped his knee, thoroughly enjoying his position of power. "And when can I meet this woman who has captured the elusive Edmond Gregory?"

I glanced toward the door. "Soon. But listen, I need a favor."

"Another favor," he whistled. "I must say, I like you in love."

"I need to slip out right after dinner. Can you cover for me?"

He nodded. "Sure. I'll say you need to go with me to the brothel."

"Something else," I groaned.

"To church?"

"Jerome!"

"Okay," he sighed. "I'll tell him we're headed to the tavern tonight. Do you need to slip out for a little carnal knowledge?"

"Something like that," I nodded. "And thank you, brother."

"You're welcome, Father."

SISTER ELIZABETH

J didn't agree to get rid of the priest in Ipswich because of the threats made, both directly and indirectly, by Bishop Gregory. No, I would have done this task with no incentive, with no motive, other than to free at least one church of an abusive clergyman.

Late the next morning, I joined the crowd at the large cathedral disguised as an altar boy. The elderly Father Ryland's vision had deteriorated to the extent that in the dim candlelight, I passed easily as one of his normal prey. My short stature and lean frame, plus the crude wig I wore, was enough for him not to notice me slipping in alongside the pack of altar boys.

But, of course, *they* knew. The young men could tell that I was not one of them, but none seemed to care. Glassy eyed, they roamed the large cathedral, going about their duties and desperately trying to avoid being the next one chosen by the predator that ran the city.

Bishop Gregory had warned me that Father Ryland was powerful, and had ruled that parish for the past twenty years. *Twenty years* of hell for the people of Ipswich. And yet, they obeyed. The girls escaped for the most part, but doing time alongside the evil priest was just a rite of passage for most of the males.

One of the altar boys, Christopher, pulled me aside quickly. "Did the pope send you?"

I was confused. "The pope?"

"You're a woman, an adult! Surely God has answered my prayers."

"Oh, yes, of course. Please tell no one that I'm here observing."

"No, never. I knew this day would come. I've prayed daily for salvation from *him*."

"Father Ryland?"

"Yes. I'm his favorite," the boy, not much older than thirteen, said. His eyes searched the floor as a wave of shame drifted across his face.

"He touches you?"

"And beyond," he said, never looking me in the eye.

"Have you told your father?"

The boy laughed, as if the idea was absurd. "Maybe they could have you released from service. You seem old enough to escape this hell."

"My parents *want* me here. They know *everything*."

I wanted to be shocked, but I wasn't. "The priest is good to them?"

He nodded. "Yes, and my father said he did *his* duty, years ago, and now it is my turn."

I nodded at the boy. "Christopher, can you help me find a way to be alone with the priest later?"

"Oh, you mustn't! No, I will protect you."

"God will protect me. I have been sent by Him to answer your prayers!"

He smiled wide, his eyes meeting mine for the first time. "Praise Him!"

"Help me to be alone with the old monster, and I shall bring justice from on high."

~

After mass, the entire congregation fled in terror. It was nothing like Father Gregory's services had been in Worthington. There was no talk of hope, no respite from the grim lives of the parishioners; no, this priest only talked of hell.

Within in an hour after the candles being extinguished, the foul-smelling old man shuffled across the stones toward the only ones remaining – his army of young altar boys. He looked around, as if choosing, while none of them made eye contact. But the brave Christopher stepped out with a luscious grin.

"Perhaps you'd like to chose two of us today, Father?"

The decrepit old man approached, squeezing his heavy eyelids together as if to see better. Christopher reached for my shoulder, bringing me to his side. "Another yellow-haired slim boy, Father. Shall we give him a try?"

The monster sniffed me, and his curled, yellow fingernail touched my face. "He smells fresh!"

Christopher looked at me and winked. "Yes, Father, young and new to the area. He's very much afraid."

The grotesque man inhaled deeply, titillated by the idea of a new conquest, and even better, one who was in fear. "Yes, follow," he said, releasing the others with the wave of his hand. They fled like rats from a sinking ship, relieved to be spared that day.

We followed behind the slow-moving, heavily robed old man until we were alone in his private quarters. "Get the oil, Christopher, and have this boy disrobe."

"Lie back, Father, let me show him." Christopher looked to me again before extinguishing all but one of the candles.

Father Ryland pawed at his robes, his movements slow. "Come now, boy, don't be afraid. It'll only hurt a little."

I approached, the steel of the blade causing my fingers to twitch in anticipation of a kill. "It'll hurt *a lot* when I slice off your cock," I said in his ear as I hovered over him.

Alarmed, he began to shake. "Who are you? What did you dare say to me? Christopher, help!"

"I am the angel of death, and I have come to send you straight to hell." I reached under his heavy robes, my cold blade at his testicles before he could move. "This is how the Bishop Gregory deals with those who abuse the holy orders!"

"No, it's a mistake, I am innocent. This boy seduced me!"

"Christopher, go," I said, glancing over my shoulder. "You don't want to see this."

The boy, who that day truly became a man, laughed from behind us. "I want to witness every scream, every drop of blood. For the others and myself, and all those that came before us, I will savor his torture."

With a quick slice, I castrated the filthy, stinking vermin.

"Let it be that, let it only be that," he begged.

"Oh no, we've just begun." Slice after slice, justice was done.

Finally, I was drawn from the euphoria of my task by the voice of my beloved.

"Sister Elizabeth, I believe that is enough. This filth has been dead for at least twenty minutes." I looked down; I was covered with blood.

"Yes, Father Gregory. I got carried away."

Edmond chuckled. "As usual, Bess. As usual."

Christopher had witnessed the entire thing, the sweet smile of revenge across his lips. "I'll tell no one," he said.

"Tell everyone." Edmond walked over to him, and with a

nod said, "Go. But tell everyone what happens to lecherous priests who prey on the young in East Anglia."

I left the corpse to wash my hands in a basin. "Clean up?" I asked, glancing to the bloody mess that used to be the priest.

"Uncle has sent reinforcements for that. You and I need to get home."

We left under cover of darkness, leaving a team of ten to wipe the blood up and dispose of the body. Well, the *pieces* of flesh that were his body.

I heard later that the city was overjoyed to be assigned a new priest, one who served the community, as a true cleric should. As far as my courageous blond accomplice that day, he was long gone by the time we emerged from the cathedral. Many years later, I did run into him again. He'd become Archbishop Christopher Radcliffe, and his mission was to scourge the Anglican Church of abusive clergy.

~

After our brush with the lecherous priest, we were left alone for the most part in the cavernous halls of the abbey. But as usual, I grew restless. A nun who'd been especially kind to me, Margaret, offered to let me accompany her on her duties.

I knew that Edmond wouldn't like me being out of the confines of the convent walls, but I went with Margaret anyway. One morning while giving out food to the poor, the news reached me. Two peasants were gossiping in the alms line.

"Did you hear she's been accused of *witchcraft*? The trial is next week," one of them said to another. She lowered her voice at the word witchcraft as if to not even dare be heard saying the abhorrent word.

I continued to hand out the extra bread as the other

answered, her voice well above a whisper. "I heard she cast a spell on her husband!"

The other nodded. "Stupid George the Wooler! He should have known better than to marry that witch."

They were talking about my father!

"Sister Elizabeth, you are needed in the vegetable garden," Joan barked from behind me.

"Yes, Mother," I answered, unable to move.

She placed her hand on my shoulder. "Go, I shall finish this."

As I turned to leave, I heard the women again. "And I heard she murdered her daughter! Burned her and the husband up in their own house!"

"The work of the devil," the other said.

"Vegetable garden, now, Sister Elizabeth!"

I ran from the gossiping women and into the abbey. I found Edmond pacing amongst the rows of vegetables.

"You have to stay inside!" he said, worry across his face. "I sent Joan out to drag you back in. You could be recognized. Worthington isn't *that* far from here."

I sat with him in the lush earth of the magnificent garden that the sisters managed. The excess that they grew was donated to the hungry, along with any other extra food from their tables. To many of the poor of the city, these alms were the only food they received.

"Sometimes I think I'll go mad inside these white walls."

He nodded. "I know, my love. It's only for a little longer, though. My uncle seems to have a plan to get you out."

"Out?"

"Out of England. Free."

"I'm not going anywhere without you."

His face was sad. "I'm working on that part."

"But first I have to go home," I said.

His head whipped toward me. "What? Seriously?"

"Seriously," I repeated, mocking Edmond's favorite word.

"Bess, you can't! Not ever!"

"My mother is being tried for witchcraft."

"I know," he said.

I bolted up and stared down at him, hands on my hips. "Did you plan to tell me?"

He rose to his feet and let out a deep breath, as if he'd been dreading this moment. "No."

"I'm going back! She's one of the few people who ever cared for me. And she's also being accused of murdering *me*!"

"Relax, Elizabeth. I have no intention of allowing harm to come to Eleanor."

"You have a plan?"

He nodded. "Yes. Bishop Gregory is presiding over the trial." Edmond shot me a wink.

"I don't trust him! Is there a jury? The townspeople hate my mother!"

Edmond reached for me, desperate to hold me. I let him take me into his arms. "I don't trust him either, but he needs you."

"Surely your uncle has others?" I asked.

"Not like you, Bess. He won't risk losing you, and saving your mother is an easy favor for him to do. On top of that, he absolutely abhors the misogyny of these witchcraft trials."

"You are sure?"

"I am sure. He's even moved her trial here to Cambridge."

"So that's why the peasants are all gossiping about it."

"Yes," he said. "But if it makes you feel better, I'll sit in on the trial as well."

"Oh please do! Save her Edmond, for me."

~

I meant to do as they wished. I *meant* to stay in the walls of the abbey, unseen. I *meant* to trust them to do as they said and find my mother innocent of the charges against her. But true to my nature, I could not sit idly by as events unfolded.

The Bishop Gregory sent his ornate carriage for Edmond and Joan the morning of my mother's trial. The Gregory Family was well respected, and Edmond thought a show of strength from all of them might influence the crowd.

What they didn't know was that in the back of the carriage, I was rolled up in a heavy blanket. I needed to see for myself.

Once the carriage stopped in the private livery, I waited until the area was empty before sneaking out. It was easy; I'd always had a knack for being stealthy. With my headdress low over my eyes, I blended in with the crowd.

From the very back of the congregation, I watched as the trial took place in the very center of town. The surge of the people was far too great for any of the churches or administrative buildings to contain.

Far in front of me, Edmond was on a makeshift wooden stage, looking positively divine in his most formal priestly robes. Joan sat in the front row, and I saw her wave to my mother as the guards walked her out.

I held my breath, terrified that the crowd would turn on her. These trials were pure spectacle, and often they turned into a violent mob. Bishop Gregory had been wise to move the proceedings away from Worthington.

I pressed forward in the crowd, desperate to hear.

Within minutes, the bishop himself came out, his long robes swishing across the stage as he greeted the onlookers. Several in front pressed to touch his feet, hoping for a blessing.

The five men gathered to be in the jury were unfamiliar to me. *Men from Cambridge, not Worthington,* I thought in relief.

The bishop spoke loudly from high atop a pedestal, his hands raised to the sky as if praying. "Good people of East Anglia, I took upon myself the unprecedented act of bringing a witch trial here to Cambridge. Why would I do such a thing?"

Bishop Gregory allowed a long pause for the crowd to absorb his words.

"Why indeed, Your Grace?" Edmond asked, his jeweled hands stretched wide, fueling the drama stirring in the already-excited crowd.

I strained to see my mother through the thicket of people. She sat in a corner chair, her face calm. She smiled at Edmond as he spoke again. "Why, my bishop, would we want to participate in such theater?"

The bishop nodded. "Theater! The perfect word."

The crowd was abuzz, unsure which side to throw their support behind.

"Now here in Cambridge, we are enlightened. We are to set an example for misguided communities like Worthington." He spat the last word, as if it were so distasteful he could barely say the name of the village.

The crowd howled, honored to be so complimented by the bishop.

Holding up his arms again to silence them, Bishop Gregory continued. "My fine nephew was this woman's village priest."

Edmond stood and bowed, the crowd clapping loudly and screaming his name. Many were enamored with the handsome young priest, son of the now-deceased wealthy Lord Gregory, nephew to the powerful Bishop of Cambridge himself.

He sat back down next to my mother and reached for her hand, a dangerous show of support for a woman accused of witchcraft.

"I myself administered the sacrament of marriage to this fine Christian's daughter, God rest her soul." Bishop Gregory made the sign of the cross, and Edmond's head fell in grief for my demise.

"Now, dear merciful people of Cambridge, let's hear from this devout woman's accuser!"

The crowd hissed. They were ready to hang someone, and thankfully it didn't seem to be my mother.

Almost pushed onto the stage by one of the magistrates, Abner Stone appeared before the crowd. The jury glared at him, spurred on by the tone of the Gregory Family.

"You accused this woman?" the bishop asked.

"I-er-um, ah…"

"And now it seems you are mute?"

The crowd howled in laughter. Edmond leaned in and whispered to my mother, who nodded her head in response.

"Abner Stone, did you or did you not publicly accuse this God-fearing woman of a crime most severe?"

"I did," the red-faced villain said.

"Fine, then," the Bishop said, taking his seat and leaving Abner to stand.

The vengeful Abner Stone stood there, unsure of what to do. In Worthington, everyone would have stood in a circle and, for no other reason than hatred for my mother, they would have howled, thrown things, and dragged her to the river for the "witch trial." Of course, if she floated she was a witch, and if she drowned, well, of course, she would be found innocent – posthumously.

Abner looked to the jury, and then to the bishop. He was lost and confused. The day wasn't going as he'd imagined. "She cast a spell on my friend, George the Wooler. He told me. And on top of that, she'd been poisoning him for years."

I wanted to scream *Liar!* My father, evil as he was, hated the horrid man who now stood on stage, accusing my mother. Of course, the poisoning part was true, but my father knew Mother was no witch. She was simply a resourceful apothecary.

The bishop stared at the man, and after a long pause, said, "Your evidence, sir. Present your evidence."

Abner stammered, looking to the crowd for support. He found none. They screamed the word in response, "Evidence!"

"Oh, there is no evidence." Edmond stood up and walked toward the crowd. He nodded at several women in front, who blushed and giggled at the attention from the handsome priest. "You thought," he continued, "that these just, honest men would put an innocent woman to death based on your word only?"

The throng of people jeered at Abner.

"*You* know, Father Gregory! You were there when her daughter and the good man, John the Brewer, went up in hell fire!"

Edmond looked to the ground. "I know that a tragedy occurred and that this woman, Eleanor Darby, lost both her husband and her child in one night. And now, you put her here through *this*."

The crowd went from merely verbally berating Abner to throwing garbage at him.

Edmond held up his hand to quiet the crowd. "Abner Stone, is it not true that you wanted this woman for your own, and she rejected you? Isn't that the true reason for this accusation?"

"No! That's a lie. The Darby women are *all* witches!"

Bishop Gregory stood and gestured toward my mother. "Shall we put this distasteful accusation to the vote of the fair, merciful men of our jury?"

Again, the crowd howled, but they howled *for* my mother. "Free her! Put her accuser on the pillory! Justice!" they chanted. Relieved, I relaxed for the first time in days. And then he saw me. Edmond's eyes locked onto mine, the color draining from his face.

He whispered to his uncle and made his way from the stage. My first instinct was to run like a child caught doing wrong. I weaved through the agitated crowd, fighting my way back to the livery. Irrationally, I thought I could hide in the carriage and avoid the anger of my beloved.

But as soon as I'd closed the heavy livery door, I sensed I wasn't alone. Richard Stone, the son of my mother's accuser and the one who'd attacked me in the woods that day, stood before me. In his hands was a heavy iron tool. He was about to loosen the carriage wheels.

When he saw me, his face turned red with rage. "I knew you weren't dead!"

"I am dead," I said calmly, smoothing my tunic. "And I'm about to take you with me."

The monster walked toward me with the iron bar raised. "Then we're about to go straight to hell!"

"Like your father? Lying fool that he is."

"Your mother is a witch."

"And you are an idiot. I should have castrated you when I had the chance."

He came closer. It would do me no good to scream – the crowd was again roaring outside. Even if shouting for help was an option, I couldn't risk being seen.

"You *should* have castrated me," he said, one hand tugging at the laces of his trousers. "I've never spilled my seed into a nun before."

He dropped the iron bar and lurched forward, his hulking size bearing down on me. As soon as was near enough, however, my blade sliced through his grotesque penis, blood spurting as the severed tip landed in the dirty sawdust.

Shock set in, as it usually did. Without missing a beat, I

jammed my knife into his ribs, twisting it until he fell to the ground. "Giant men are often so stupid and weak," I said. With another jab, my knife sank into his bowels. Unable to control the rage I felt toward this rapist, I disemboweled him while he was still alive.

I cut, and I cut, and I cut. Long after he was dead, my knife still bore my rage. I sliced at the corpse until a hand was on my shoulder, pulling me away.

"Blood again! God Bess, why can you not learn to kill with less *mess*?"

I shrugged. "I was angry."

"Seriously!" Edmond said.

We heard voices, and Edmond gestured toward the carriage. Before the creaky door opened, I was hidden in the blanket.

I heard several men talking loudly, and then the voice of Bishop Gregory. "Clean this up, Clarence," the bishop said, as if bored. As if a bloody, butchered body were an every day occurrence.

"Yes, Your Grace," the voice said.

I could barely hear the muffled voice of Edmond. "He attacked me, tried to sabotage our carriage. What else was I supposed to do, Uncle?"

"What indeed," the bored voice of Bishop Gregory said.

Once the carriage was rolling, the noise of the city behind us, I could heard them speaking. "I'll send your men a cask of wine for the trouble of the messy cleanup," Edmond said.

"They shall appreciate it," the bishop replied. "Now she owes me another favor, don't you dear?"

"This was my doing. I just happened to have her knife in my—"

"Bollocks," the bishop said. "Am I correct, Sister Elizabeth?" he shouted toward the back of the carriage.

"Yes, sir," I said, climbing out of the rolled up blanket to sit next to Edmond and his sister on the bench.

"Mother was freed?"

Bishop Gregory nodded. "But of course. I gave Edmond my word. The jury was entirely made up of my men."

"And Abner? Do you think he'll accuse us of Richard's disappearance?"

"Disappearance," Edmond said with a chuckle. "More like a butchering."

The bishop looked at me. "I'm sure our lovely assassin was simply defending herself. Yes?"

I nodded. "Yes. He tried to rape me. Again!"

"Well, then you should have taken care of him the first time. Never suffer a rapist to live. But no, Abner Stone will say nothing. In fact, he met an unfortunate accident on his way back to Worthington."

"How do you know? We left right after the—"

"He knows because he set it up, Bess. Neither father nor son was ever going to make it back home alive."

～

"May I have my knife back?" I asked late that night in the darkness.

Edmond rolled over toward me, his bare skin on mine. "You have not been a good girl today, Sister Elizabeth."

"I had no choice."

"You can choose to work more efficiently."

"Less blood."

His fingertips stroked my cheek. "A lot less blood, yes."

"I'll try."

"And a little more trust."

"I don't trust him."

"No, but you can trust me. I love you, Bess."

"I love you, too. I'm just not used to being loved."

His lips brushed my cheek. "Get used to it, because I'm going to love you a lot, and forever."

"I love the sound of forever."

When he sank in to me, nothing else mattered. That night, when he and I were one, the universe faded into oblivion. Our love, we two, was strong enough to mute any army, any nation. Love would be all, and as we came together countless times in the night, I knew that despite the war in front of us, Edmond and I would transcend. Somehow, someway; it had to be.

EDMOND

"Surely we can do more for them," I said to Joan one afternoon, the witch trial behind us.

"Soft-hearted Edmond."

I shook my head. "No, I'm certainly not. But we live like kings while the orphans live like rats. Surely the abbey could build a facility for them?"

"The poor you will always have with you, that's what the Book says."

I could not have cared less what the Good Book said. I *did* care about the hungry children that lived in squalor at the walls of the great Stoneham Abbey. "You know full well, Sister, what that quote was referring to."

From the corner, my brilliant Elizabeth spoke up. She quoted, "For the poor you will always have with you in the land. Therefore I command you, 'You shall open wide your hand to your brother, to the needy and to the poor, in your land.' Deuteronomy, yes?"

"Yes," I said. "Let's open wide our hands. At least for the children, Joan."

"My life was far simpler before you two," she said, but

there was a smile on her face. "What do you need from me?"

"Food. Gold. Compassion," I answered.

"Compassion I have, food we're giving what we can. Gold, however, is in short supply."

Elizabeth stood up and walked to the window. "Our dog eats better than most of those children."

"Your dog is a nuisance, as are those children." Ursula stood at the door, her perpetual sneer on her face.

"Now Sister Ursula." Joan walked over and took her by the hand. "Perhaps we should be more charitable."

"I don't see much Gregory money flowing toward the poor," Ursula snapped.

"Ursula!" Joan pulled her hand away as if burned.

"No, she's right." Edmond stood and paced the floor. "We are privileged, yes. We want for nothing. Except...money. Our brother controls the family purse. To build an orphanage, we'd need financing."

"Perhaps the bishop?"

I shook my head at Elizabeth. "Charity is not his strong suit. Besides, all of his funds are tied up in the palatial estate he's building in London."

I paced the floor. Elizabeth spoke from the window. "Surely the landowners around the abbey could contribute? Perhaps if compelled to?"

"Yes, that's where we shall seek funds," I agreed.

"You're suggesting that we rob Peter to pay Paul?" Joan asked.

"I'm suggesting," I said, "that we hold these titled landowners to their duty."

"And if they decline?" Joan asked.

"We don't let that be an option! And we start with the landowner to our east." I was shocked to see Ursula speak up.

"Sister Ursula, are you with us?"

She smiled at me for the first time ever. "Yes!"

"But mostly she wants to stick it to Lord Houston. He's rich enough to fund the entire endeavor." Joan shot Ursula a knowing look.

"Yes, he has been quite cruel to me," Ursula said.

"So tomorrow, someone approaches Lord Houston on behalf of the children."

"It should be me," Joan said.

Ursula walked over and wrapped her arm around Joan's waist, a rare gesture in front of others. "You know, my lovely sister, that is *must* be me."

~

Although it felt like a strange alliance indeed, the next day I rode to the massive manor house with Sister Ursula. My sister made me promise not to leave her side.

"I don't approve of your behavior, but it's not why you think," Ursula said as we stopped to water the horses.

"I don't really care. Seriously."

"Fair enough," she said. "Let's go greet the great Lord Houston."

When we reached the sprawling manor house, we were let in without hesitation. "They must trust the clergy."

"No," she answered. "They know me."

"You are full of surprises, Sister Ursula."

"Many more to come, Father Gregory."

"So they know you how, exactly?"

"I was born here."

Before I could get more information, a voice called from the corner. "Ursula!"

"Alfred!"

"I never thought I'd see you again." They embraced as if long-parted.

"We are a mile apart, and yet worlds away. Alfred, this is Father Gregory. We're here to talk to Father."

"Father?" I asked as I shook the boy's hand.

"I never thought you'd speak to him again," he said to Ursula.

"Neither did I. But the abbey has need of his resources."

Alfred laughed as he led us into the great hall. "That tight-fisted mini-monarch isn't going to part with even a farthing for the church."

"Lord Houston is going to build an orphanage, as well as donate the land it will sit on."

"And who is going to convince him of that? Father Gregory here?"

She shook her head. "He will do it for me."

Alfred led us through the hall and to the rear, toward the family's private rooms. "Father!" he called out. "Ursula has come home."

An obese man burst from a heavy door, straightening his coat as the men behind him clamored to keep up with their Lord. "Home?"

"No, Your Grace. I have come for a visit."

"Ah, so you still serve God, I see," the man said with disdain.

"Yes, and the abbess."

Lord Houston cringed. "Unclean and unnatural."

Ursula looked to her younger brother. "May I speak with Lord Houston in private?"

With the wave of his hand, the man begrudgingly emptied the room and we were alone. "Sit," he commanded.

He poured a cup of ale, offering us nothing. "What do you want?"

Ursula straightened her habit, making the man wait. When she was ready she began. "Sister Joan, our Reverend

Mother, has bestowed upon you the honor of being the benefactor of the new orphanage."

He smiled and poured us each a cup of ale. "Ah, finally, the respect I deserve."

Ursula shot him a fake smile. "Deserve," she repeated.

Lord Houston grinned like a cat about to eat a mouse. I still wasn't sure why I was there, but I suspected the cunning Ursula was laying a trap for her arrogant father.

"The orphanage shall be named after you, of course."

The man smiled even wider than I thought possible. "That will be grand!"

Ursula nodded. "Of course the cost of this holy endeavor will be borne by Your Grace."

His eyes opened wide. "Surely I shall contribute a small stipend, but we cannot bear the cost of such an undertaking."

"You will."

The man blinked fast and swallowed down the rest of his second cup of ale. He poured another, leaving our cups empty. "No."

Ursula took a deep breath and sighed as if bored. "If you do not, I shall tell Father Gregory here of your sins."

The man's head snapped to me. *So that was why I was there.* I nodded, trying to look as pious as possible. "And your penance, sir, would be to confess these heinous sins publicly." I now knew her game, and was more than happy to play along to get the orphanage built.

"You would not!" he howled at her.

"I would. In fact, I'll begin now." She turned to me, and after the sign of the cross, began as if in a confessional booth. "Forgive my Father, for he has sinned. When I was ten, I watched as this man fornicated with a—"

"Stop!" The man hopped to his feet, faster than seemed humanly possible given his large size.

"Shall I bring my dear brother in to hear the rest?"

He shook, his head snapping toward the door. "Not my Alfred! You would not sully him!"

"Sully you, you mean. And you are *quite* sullied, are you not?"

Lord Houston turned to appeal to me. "Father Gregory, you must see such things happen in a household." He pointed to me. "She is always watching! Whispering, spying. Ursula was born an evil child, and now she dares to judge me."

I leaned back in my chair and poured *myself* another cup of ale. "God will judge you, Lord Houston. And further, today it has been granted by our savior that I judge you. So, would you like to publicly unburden yourself, or shall Sister Ursula do it for you? Perhaps in front of the entire congregation at the cathedral on Sunday?"

"You conspire with this woman! She *lies* with *women*, did you know that?"

"And whom do you lie with, my lord?"

"Or *what*?" Ursula asked with a snicker.

I narrowed my gaze at him, the lowest form of life. "How much?" he said, exasperated. The large man flopped back into his chair, a cloud of dust surrounding him.

"Ah, good. Now that the *unpleasantness* is over, we can talk business," I said, pulling out the plans for the new orphanage.

～

I knew the news wasn't good when I was summoned back to the bishop's palace.

"About the orphanage, we had to do it. There was no other way."

The bishop stared at me, then waved his jeweled fingers in the air. "I don't care about your blackmail of Lord Houston. That fool came to me begging for justice."

"Justice," I chuckled.

"What secret does he have that is so heinous that he would part with that amount of gold?"

"I'm not sure, exactly. I'd guess bestiality, among other wickedness."

"When he's done with orphanage, get him to build a hospital," the bishop said with a smile.

"So you're not angry? Then why the urgent summons for me to come here alone?"

He took a deep breath and gestured for me to sit. After the wine was poured, he cleared the room of his servants. "It is time for Sister Elizabeth to earn her keep."

"You swore an oath to release her when her task was done," I argued.

"Yes, Edmond," my uncle said. "But her task isn't done. Ridding the church of Father Rybalt was only a minor test, practice if you will."

"Minor?" I was about to rage at him, but fought to keep control.

He nodded. "Elizabeth's true task reaches the very crown of England. When the faith is saved from peril, only then will I arrange her escape."

The words *her escape* hit me like a horse hoof to my gut. *Her* escape.

I willed myself to be calm; I didn't want to give the bishop emotional power over me. "She can stay at the abbey, of course. Sister Elizabeth has fully absorbed her very being."

He looked at the floor and with the quick shake of his head, I knew my situation was far more complicated than I realized. "She has not, but this has nothing to do with her devotion. Rome has entrusted us with the epic task of preserving the one true faith."

"So the rumors are true?" I'd heard whispers that the king intended to form his own church, the Church of England, in order to gain the divorce that Rome repeatedly refused to grant him.

"She can't do this! It's…" I lowered my voice. "It's treason; regicide."

He nodded, an index finger to his lips. "There is no other way."

"There must be another, someone more suited for this task. And the king!" I put my hand to my forehead as the room began to swirl. "I grew up with him! Let me talk to him. Harry will listen to me."

He shook his head. "I petitioned for you to join Sister Elizabeth at court. The request was returned shredded. He has not forgiven you."

"It's too great a task for her."

"Edmond, it is not. I have seen it – it is her destiny." He lowered his voice. "She will kill the king."

"If she does this thing, what is to become of her? Of us?" That afternoon, I realized my uncle's plan was for me to go back to the clergy and she, if she were to survive, would be sent far from peril. Far from *me*.

"Edmond, you know you are like a son to me. If we can stop the king from breaking with Rome, I will be made a cardinal. That much has been sworn. You, of course, will take over the bishopric here in Cambridge. I have big plans for you, for *us*."

"If you care for me at all, release me. I don't want to serve God, I never have. Please let me go."

"I cannot," he said flatly.

The room swirled around me as I reached for the mahogany table. *I'd been such a fool!* "Then let me have her. If I cannot be free, allow me the joy of a life with Elizabeth."

"Sit," he said with the wave of his hand.

We didn't speak until we'd emptied our glasses.

"Edmond, it would be difficult."

I sensed a ray of hope. "But not impossible."

He sighed, his favorite form of expression. His jeweled fingers rubbed at his temple as he thought. "If she's able to successfully eliminate the threat to our demise completely enough, I will do my utmost to keep her safe."

"And with me," I argued.

"And with you." He took a long sip of his wine, his eyes never meeting mine. "But it will cost you."

"Of course," I chuckled. "It would be mad for you simply to want to do something for me."

"It's not that. Once the deed is done, it will be quite impossible for Sister Elizabeth to remain in England. She will have to be hidden."

"But that's easy for you!" I argued. "You do it all the time."

"True, I did once have a knack for arranging disappearances. But we both know I'm at a loss after Franco's defection."

"Defection," I said with as much of a grin as I dared. Franco was my uncle's go-to man for all things messy until the year prior when he'd disappeared in the middle of the night without warning.

"Franco, yes. From what I've heard, he was in the same sort of bind as my beloved Elizabeth."

My uncle's face looked as though he'd sucked a dozen Italian lemons.

"I saved that damnable man from a thousand tortures! Do you know how he came into my service in the first place?"

"No," I admitted. "Nor do I care."

"Well, I assure you, it's far more heinous than doing away with a monster husband. He owes me more."

"And how much more does my Elizabeth owe you?"

"If she can do this thing, she will be released from my servitude forever."

"You miss him, don't you? Franco?"

"He betrayed me!" he howled.

"You pushed too hard and someone else made him a better offer."

"Enough talk of him! Go back and prepare her for court life. Teach her all she needs to know, and make sure King Henry believes that she is your long-lost cousin Elizabeth."

"How long do I have?" I could not imagine teaching even the brilliant Elizabeth all the ins and outs of court life.

"A month or so, maybe less. Rome is pressuring me like no other."

"It's not going to be easy."

"Understatement of the century," he agreed with a nod. "But I have a feeling about her. It is her destiny."

"Her place is with me!"

He sighed again, shaking his head in exasperation.

~

That night she slipped into my bed.

"My love, you didn't come to me after vespers. Are you ill?"

I rolled over to face her and wound my fingers through her hair. "No, my love. Merely troubled."

"Don't be, Edmond. The orphanage is going to be a huge success."

I nodded.

"Was the bishop angry? Is that was this is about?" Her fingertips stroked my cheek. I didn't know how to tell her.

"No, he wasn't angry at all."

"But he called you to Cambridge today?"

"Yes," I nodded.

We held each other in silence for several long minutes. Finally, I began. I told her the entire thing; of the impossible mission she'd been tasked with. Of the things I must teach her. Of the immense peril she would be in.

"Of course I will succeed," she said confidently.

"Bess, this isn't like the other things you've done. The king is surrounded by guards at all times, it's not as if you'll sneak into his chambers and simply eliminate him."

Her lips kissed my chest. "Does our monarch even deserve such a thing?"

"Deserve is a strong word." I thought of the many men that Henry, and his father before him, had put to death to seize the throne.

"Do you want him dead?"

"No," I admitted. "But we have to find a way to be free, and to be together."

"I'll move heaven and earth to be with you, Edmond Gregory."

My lips fell onto hers and as her thighs opened to me, I knew we'd find a way.

～

By day, I trained Elizabeth on the ins and outs of court life.

She was a fast learner, as always. Her French wasn't great, but King Henry tended to use English and her Latin was impeccable. She was far more educated than most nuns, and certainly more than my dead cousin had been. As far as manners, she was able to master those by extensive practice and drills from Joan and me.

By the end of the month, I was convinced she'd be able to blend in once she was sent to London. What I wasn't sure of, however, was how she would get close to the king. Disguised as a nun, it would be hard for even my beautiful Bess to catch his eye.

One morning as we were walking in the courtyard, I

decided it was time to talk of matters of the flesh, and of the heart. "Bess, there's more than just passing as a nun in the chapel royal. You will need to get close to him."

She nodded. "I know. How do I do that?"

"You'll need to seduce him." I said the words as if it was a perfectly ordinary thing to say to the woman you loved.

"I will not!"

I scratched my head, pondering on the best way to approach the subject further. "The way to the king is through his heart...and his bed."

"Edmond!" She turned to me. "I don't want to know another man but you."

"Don't want to?"

She looked confused. "Well, don't intend to. It's a sin, is it not?"

I resisted the urge to take her in my arms. There were far too many spying eyes around for that. "I don't believe what God created to be sin. Do you feel it is a sin between us? Our closeness?"

"No," she said. "For I love you. If I could be, I would be your wife."

I nodded. "Yes. You will be, when we are free. However, the pleasure of the flesh with others between us may not be quite so...evil as you think."

She continued to walk, deep in her thoughts.

"Elizabeth," I said after several minutes. "To live, you may need to lie with the king. Further, you may even grow to love him."

She didn't answer, but I could see the struggle of her conscience. "I will never love another as I do you."

"Nor I you," I said. "When you go to court, do your best to catch the eye of the king. Do not, however, harm him. Not until you hear from me, my love."

"Do you have a plan?" I saw the sparkle in her eye.

"I do."

~

As I was busy training Elizabeth for her impossible task, the orphanage broke ground. Sadly, however, our good graces from Ursula did not last. Only weeks after our visit to Lord Gregory, I heard Ursula's shrill voice complaining to my sister. I waited in the shadows, listening.

"Joan, he's trouble, and that little witch *he* brought here has to go. Let me take care of her."

My sister, Joan, answered, "Do not speak of my brother again."

The other voice sighed loudly. "Fine. But that little whore he's bedding *has* to go! She puts us *all* in jeopardy!"

My fingers flexed; I wanted to strangle whoever would dare speak of my Elizabeth in such a way.

"Ursula, he loves her as I love you. I do share your worries about their presence here, however."

Damn Sister Ursula! I knew she was trouble.

"He'll find another, my love. Let me get rid of the girl. The Friar showed me how to—"

"The Friar would have killed you himself if I didn't intervene! No Ursula, I demand that you stay far from this business."

"You never choose me first!" Ursula shouted.

She fled the room and blew past me in the hallway without a glance. When she was out of sight, I rounded the corner into my sister's room. "Someone is not happy," I said with a shake of my head.

Joan forced a smile. "Ah, Ursula. She certainly can lean toward the dramatic."

"But you love her?"

"I do," she said.

"Will she try to harm Elizabeth? Because I would highly advise against it. Sister Elizabeth is like none I've seen since the Friar."

"So I've heard." She gestured toward the table. "Wine? Because I need wine right now." She sat in the simple wooden chair and filled our glasses.

I sat across from her. "Elizabeth has a strong talent, but she doesn't know how to control it yet. She lacks discipline and experience."

"And yet, it seems Rome has quite an epic task for her."

"She's not ready, Sis. There's no way she can get to a king, do this thing, *and* get out alive."

Joan took a long sip of her wine. "Are you sure, Edmond, that getting her out alive is of any concern to our dear uncle?"

I grimaced, as she'd just confirmed my worst fear. "I shall get her out alive."

"You must," she nodded. "For I have never seen you so happy."

"Does Ursula really make you happy?"

She shook her head. "No, but yet, I cannot seem to deny myself of her."

"I confess I was listening outside earlier. Did Franco really train Ursula?"

She chuckled. "No. He showed her a few things and true to her nature, she abused the power. She's still breathing because I begged him to spare her life."

"You may regret that decision." I took another sip of the French wine.

"Don't! I love her; I need her. There's good in there."

I stared at her, one eyebrow raised.

"Somewhere!" she laughed.

"Be careful, Joan. I'll do anything for Elizabeth."

"And I for you."

"To family," I said with a raised glass.

～

Late that night, Elizabeth's head was on my bare chest. "Edmond, do you really think she's a threat?"

"I know she is. I heard the venom in her voice."

"I'll get rid of Ursula, no problem. Don't think twice about it." Her fingertips ran across my chest and I knew I'd have to have her again before we slept. Once was never enough, and often twice was just the beginning.

"I need you to leave Ursula be," I told her, my hands running down her naked back. "I promised Joan."

"They are lovers?"

"Yes." My fingers dipped lower, down the small of her back.

"I'd only heard rumors of such things, and to see it happen in the abbey bewilders me." She looked up at me, the face of an angel waiting for my answer.

"Those things happen *especially* in the abbey. But Bess, you must open your mind to things that you learned were evil."

"I am, Edmond, I truly am."

"I know, my darling. Joan has always loved women, in that way. It is not something she chooses. It is no more sin than what we share."

"And yet, she *chose* to become a nun? Unlike you, she had a choice?"

I wrapped my arms around her waist and rolled her over. I needed her again.

"She did. I believe it was her way to never be forced to be something she was not."

"Ah, I see," she said as our bodies joined.

ELIZABETH

I expected it to be Ursula, but it was ultimately Joan who ended up pushing me out.

"You cannot stay," she said one rainy afternoon.

"I will not leave Edmond. I'm not ready!"

She smiled, her face softening. "Please sit."

"Yes, Reverend Mother."

"Call me Joan, please, while we are alone. We are practically family."

"Well then, Joan, why does my new family choose to throw me out of the safety of God's own dwelling and into the mouth of the wolves?" I thought I'd have more time, but it seemed I was running out of luck.

She removed her headdress and shook her long auburn hair free. "It isn't my choice, Elizabeth. Now that the court has returned from summer progress, Cardinal Wolsey demands that the chapel be fully served. My uncle has bribed him to secure your place at court, and the cardinal demands that you join them before Michaelmas."

"So suddenly the king cares about religious traditions!"

She urged me to be quiet. "I wish there was more I could do, but it's time for you to earn your keep."

"And Edmond? What is his role?"

She couldn't look at me while she answered. "Edmond's role is to stay here and pray that you return to him."

"I'm not sure Edmond prays."

Her fingertips went to her lips. "You know him well."

I stared into my wine, waiting for more bad news. "How long do I have?"

"A week, maybe less."

"I'm not ready!" I argued. "I know so little about how to behave as a lady. Can we have a few extra weeks?"

"It's not possible. Besides, as a nun you will stay in the fringes. You'll pass well enough. Getting close to Harry will be difficult, however, even for one as stealthy as yourself."

"Harry?" I was confused, as usual, in this strange new world.

"King Henry. We knew him when he was a lad. Back then, he was merely jolly Prince Harry to us."

"Then Edmond *must* come! He will be my way in." I saw a ray of hope in my dire situation.

But Joan looked at her hands again. "He cannot. Henry banned him from his presence years ago. He'd be immediately taken to the Tower."

"Why? Why was he banished?"

Her eyes, once again, never met mine. "I do not know," she lied.

∼

I searched the abbey grounds for Edmond, desperate to find a way not to leave him. As the rain poured, my habit became so wet I brazenly discarded it in the thick grass. "Father Gregory!" I shouted. When I'd become so soaked that even my under-clothes clung to me, I abandoned the formality and howled, "Edmond!" into the downpour.

"Bess!"

I looked around, shielding my eyes from the rain, and saw him at the door of the small gardener's cottage. I ran to him, falling into his warm arms as he bolted the door behind me. "I was out walking when it started," he said, leading me toward the fire.

My entire body shook as he peeled the wet clothes from me. When I was naked, he wrapped me in his dry robe.

"You are freezing," he said, searching the small place of refuge for something to warm me. "Ah, this will have to do," he said, finding a flask of ale on a shelf. "I'll warm it."

When he was satisfied that it was ready, he held the liquid to my lips. "Your color's coming back. What were you doing out there?"

"I needed to find you. They are sending me to court."

"Yes, I know."

"No, I mean *soon*. Joan told me just now that I'm to leave within the week."

He sat next to me as we passed the flask between us.

"Elizabeth, there is no choice. You have to go. Your mission to kill the king is the *only* thing keeping you alive right now."

"Shall I do it then?"

"No," he shook his head. "Wait for me. But get close to him, as we've discussed, in the ways I've *shown* you."

I blushed a deep scarlet. "Those were the best lessons."

He grinned. "Those holding the strings to our freedom and safety must believe that you are at task, that you will complete the mission. If they sense any form of wavering, they'll eliminate you. They may even eliminate all who know of the plot. This burden does not come from my uncle, Bess.

It comes from far higher. We are truly stuck between a rock and a hard place."

"Can we not just disappear?"

He shook his head. "No, those who would seek us out are powerful. We cannot untangle from this on our own, but I do have an idea. For now, appear to do as they wish you to."

"Appear?"

"Yes. Get close to Henry, but wait until you hear from me before you act. Do you promise?"

I nodded. "Yes. But why can you not come to court with me? I cannot bear to be away from you for even one night."

"Ah, my love," he said, reaching for my hands. "Nor I from you. But we must. We are making a play for forever, and this is our escape act."

"Joan said you were banned from court."

"Yes."

"Why?"

He didn't answer, his lips forming a hard line. "I can't lie to you, dear Bess, but you wouldn't understand just now. Will you trust me to not answer that yet?"

"I trust you with everything, Edmond."

He smiled, the relieved smile of one who skirted out of a difficult explanation.

"Go to court, and stay out of trouble. I will find a way to come to you."

"If I must," I sulked.

"Oh, and Bess, try not to kill anyone," he said with a wide smile.

"I shall try."

~

I fought the tears the morning they came for me. Compliments of the newly named Cardinal Reginald Gregory, I was to be awarded a place in the flamboyant Tudor court. Twenty minutes was all I was given to gather my things and say my goodbyes.

I only had one goodbye, and it nearly broke me.

My fingers wrapped through a ringlet of his dark curls as he held me close. It had become my habit to soothe myself in Edmond's thick hair. Often, he'd threaten to cut it, and I would beg him not to. "Shall I be like Samson? Weakened if I cut my locks?" he would tease.

"I shall never be Delilah," I said once.

But that ugly day, not even his silken curls could soothe my pain. "I shall die without your touch." Heavy teardrops fell from my eyes as his lips brushed my forehead.

"Be brave, Bess."

"I am *always* brave."

"Yes, yes you are." He kissed me until my body pressed into his. Pulling away from me, he scolded, "There's no time for that now. Go to court, remember what I taught you, and do anything to win the affection of the king."

"But stay my hand? Are we sure on this?"

"Yes, my darling. And I shall miss you bitterly."

"Oh my love, I have never needed another as I need you. I love you."

Sniffing, I kissed him once more as he bid me goodbye. "And I love you. Forever."

PART III
THE COURT OF KING
HENRY, AUTUMN, 1524

ELIZABETH

I cried all the way to court. For two days, I did nothing but ride and cry. Leaving Edmond was by far the hardest thing I'd ever done. But, when I arrived at the majestic walls of the palace, I dried my tears. There was work to be done.

The first few days at court were miserable. The other sisters and even the priests resented my presence. Each time I tried to play out my role in the chapel, I was told that they had all of the tasks under their control. I was allowed to do nothing. I wrote to Edmond of my plight, in the cryptic way he'd taught me.

One afternoon, unseasonably warm for mid-September, I sat in the gardens with my head in my hands. I had not come close to the king, and saw very little hope of doing so. Even at mass, he was hidden in his own chambers. I missed Edmond, and saw no way to get back to him.

I stood to go when a dark robed figure approached me.

"Sister Elizabeth! It's been so many years."

I gulped. My biggest fear was being questioned for details about my identity. Edmond and Joan had both told me everything they could think of about their cousin, but with a thorough questioning, my deception would be evident.

I took a gamble. "I *am* sorry, Your Grace. My memory escapes me…?"

The man smiled and nodded. "No, of course. You were but a child when we met last. I am Thomas More."

"Sir Thomas More, of course! Utopia was one of the first texts I read in Latin." My cheeks instantly grew warm; I'd blurted out information that most men of the court or otherwise would find shocking.

He gasped, and then smiled warmly again. "Excellent! I truly am honored, Sister."

I nodded, unsure of what to say.

"Shall we walk?" he asked.

I took his arm, and we strolled the gardens, all eyes on us. "Who taught you Latin, Sister Elizabeth?"

"My dear, er, my cousin, Father Gregory." Another gamble; another silent prayer that it would work.

He nodded. "Yes! I heard that young Edmond was teaching women. I highly approve."

"You do?"

"Yes! To follow God, knowledge is of the utmost importance. My wife and all of my daughters can read and write various languages."

We walked while talking philosophy and literature for over an hour that warm afternoon. Sir Thomas More was the first bright spot I'd found at court. "Ah, the hour grows late," he finally said.

"Yes, I must get back to the chapel. I do wish we could speak of such things again, Your Grace?"

"I'd truly enjoy that, Sister. How has court life been for you?"

"Difficult," I admitted.

He nodded, opening the grand door into the palace. "I

spend as little time here as possible. I'm only here today to dine with the king this evening. He's summoned me to render my opinion, once again, on the question of his marriage."

"May God be with you," I said.

~

The very next day, everything changed for me at court. I was summoned to the great hall for an audience with the king himself.

With my head down, I waited at the rear of the giant hall for two hours while the king and his mistress, who sat on the throne next to him as if she were already crowned queen, greeted those new to court.

At last, late in the afternoon, I was brought forward. "Sister Elizabeth Gregory, cousin of the Cardinal Gregory of Cambridge, has joined the royal chapel in service of Your Majesty," the announcer informed the king.

"Cardinal is he?" the larger-than-life king bellowed. "I wonder what he promised almighty Rome to get *that* advancement? Do you know, Sister?"

I moved forward slowly, my eyes only on the stone floor in front of me. Edmond told me that nobility never hurries, and that I must always bear the grace of the highborn no matter what occurred.

"I do not, Your Majesty," I said, dipping into a low curtsy just as I'd been taught in our countless hours of practice.

"Ah dear Sister, we welcome you to our court. Our closest friend, Sir Thomas More, informed us only last evening of your arrival."

I allowed my eyes to meet those of the ominous King Henry.

"Majesty, I am truly honored to join the service of our Lord."

His bright blue eyes locked with mine, and I willed my heart to cease thumping in my chest. There was no time for fear, so I set it aside as I always did when a mission was at hand.

"You've changed quite a lot since we were children," he said with a tilt of his head. "Please, approach us."

With a deep breath, I stepped toward him, without urgency as I'd been taught. He took my hand in his, his predatory eyes sweeping me up and down.

"That was years ago," I said, interrupting his lecherous sweep over my hidden body.

"True, true," he conceded, never letting go of my hand. "But something is greatly changed about you."

I waited, not blushing, not shaking. I waited, willing my entire being to be calm. This was a test; the first of many. I knew from Edmond that the king hadn't seen Lady Elizabeth Gregory since she was twelve, and that we bore a strong resemblance. Despite this, I knew that if the quiz were too in-depth, I would be exposed as an imposter. And I knew what was done with imposters.

With a bite of my lower lip and a softening of my eyes, I tilted my head. Instinct told me he was interested. Further, Anne Boleyn, pouting next to him like a spoiled child, pulled my hand from the king's.

"Thank you Sister, that will be all," she snapped.

My eyes never left Henry's. "We shall speak later," the king finally said.

"Yes, Majesty, I would like that very much." I curtseyed once again, and backed away from the presence of the mighty king.

From the corner of the throne room, I could see Anne Boleyn's dark eyes boring into me. Her grasp on the king was tight, especially with his true wife, Catherine of Aragon, sequestered far away under, for all purposes, house arrest. But that afternoon, I knew there was wiggle room between Henry and his mistress.

Many times, as the afternoon of greetings and petitions wore on, his eyes sought out my own. There was a connection. When he rose to leave, I slowly licked my lips for his benefit and he nodded. My message was clear, and the king was receptive.

But the king didn't send for me that night, or the next. So I waited, confident and terrified that I'd have my chance. Days later, late in the night, the king's own Gentleman of the Privy Chamber knocked on my door.

"Sister, His Majesty the King needs to speak with you this evening on a spiritual matter," he said with a wink.

"Surely one of the more experienced sisters would be more suitable?"

"My Lord asks for you, and you only."

The boy was thin and young – but as the keeper of his inner quarters, most powerful at court. I followed him through the back of the palace in what seemed like an endless maze of passages and doors. "You mustn't be seen," he warned. "Even the king must be discreet in these matters."

I nodded. It was show time, and I knew what I must do.

But when I arrived in the king's inner quarters, the room was full of courtiers. All were men, but we were very much *not* alone.

"Ah, Thomas, here she is." The king reached a large hand to me.

"Yes, Harry, I thought we might further our discussion of Aristotle with you?"

The king raised one eyebrow quizzically at me. "Beautiful *and* smart, Thomas? God is indeed smiling on us tonight."

We dined in the outer chamber amongst the men, and

afterward played cards and drank wine. Both men were intrigued by the reading I'd done. Throughout the course of the long evening they pestered me with questions of religion, politics, and philosophy. When the king tired, he rose to walk me to the door.

He leaned in close and whispered in my ear. "Who are you?"

Eyes wide, I looked at him, terrified. *He knew!*

"Don't worry, Sister, your secret is safe with me." With a wink, I was handed over to one of his gentlemen to be escorted back to my chambers.

That night, I paid a messenger of the court one of the gold coins given to me by Edmond. As instructed, I didn't seal the letter with wax.

"They'll read it anyway," he'd told me during our endless hours of preparation. "Just make sure the message sounds benign. I'll know your true meaning."

"Of course you will," I'd answered. "For we are soul mates."

~

The very next day, the round, red-robed figure of Cardinal Wolsey burst into the side chapel. "You will fail!" he howled.

"Your Eminence, what do you speak of?" I continued to light the candles, willing my hand not to shake. Edmond had warned me that Wolsey was dangerous. Not only was he close to the king, he had such a tight grip on the court that many said it was he who ruled, not Henry.

The Cardinal grabbed me by the elbows, whipping me around so quickly that the flame went out on the candle I was holding. "Whose side are you on, exactly?"

"The side of God, of course."

With a tightening of his grip on my arm, his eyes

narrowed at me. "I don't know who you are, but if you derail my plans for—"

"Your plans for what?" the deep voice behind us asked.

"Harry!" Wolsey let go of my arms and spun around to address the king.

I lowered into a deep curtsey. "Majesty," I said, my eyes on the ground.

Wolsey stuttered, "Y-Y-Yes *Your Majesty*, we were simply discussing..."

"You, Wolsey, were bullying this beautiful, young sister. Were you not?"

King Henry stood in front of us, his massive form towering over the both of us. His muscled arms strained at the fur of his garment as his hands went to his hips. "Sister Elizabeth, what is this about?" he asked.

I willed myself to be calm, and when I rose and my eyes met his, I felt no fear. Despite the blustery storm that he was, inside there was a good man. Lost, but honest and true. "Sire, the cardinal was about to tell me about his plans."

Wolsey sputtered but Henry signaled for him to be silent.

"Plans for what, my lady?"

"We did not get that far," I said, rubbing my arms for effect. "But he seemed agitated."

The king turned toward Wolsey. "Leave us," he said. "And do not put your withered old hands on her perfect flesh again."

"Yes, sire," Wolsey said in a growl, fleeing the chapel.

"Shall we walk?" Henry asked, stretching out his hand to me.

He led me outside, toward the long gallery that spanned the side of the palace. "You were sent here by...?" he asked.

"My uncle, Cardinal Gregory."

"Gregory..." he repeated, as if it were a prayer. "For what purpose?"

"To learn the ways of court, I believe. So I can be of service to God."

He spun around to face me, his hand on my shoulder. "They plot against me, Elizabeth." I noted that he'd now dropped the *Sister* part.

My eyes met his—deep blue, sparkling, intelligent eyes. This was not a man to beguile. "Yes, Your Majesty."

"Call me Henry, please."

"Yes, Henry, I've learned that much about court. It is hard to know whom to trust."

"When did you last see Edmond?"

The question caught me off guard. I'd learned to stick to as close to the truth as possible. "The night before I was sent away to court."

He nodded. "And you love him?"

Again, I was caught completely off guard by this straight-talking monarch. "Of course, Henry."

He smiled wide. "Finally! An honest soul in this nest of wasps!" He laughed out loud, and I laughed with him. It was hard not to, his intensity was contagious.

When the laughter stopped, he gestured for me to sit next to him on a bench. I reached for his hand, a gesture so fast, so natural I gave it no thought. Only after he squeezed my hand did I remember that I wasn't supposed to touch someone of royal blood.

"My scheming mistress is determined to see you go, as is Wolsey. I'll protect you the best that I can, but this is a dangerous place."

"Why?"

"Why is it dangerous?" he asked.

"No. Why would you protect me?"

He leaned toward me. "Because I want you. Those brown eyes, that perfect skin—it's all I've thought about since I first set eyes on you."

I felt my heart pound in my chest. "Henry, I am but a chaste maid, a servant of God, and shall remain so…"

He laughed again and shook his head. "You are neither, my girl, you are neither. And, you are *not* Elizabeth Gregory."

Before I could answer, he pulled me to my feet. "Let us walk into dinner."

"Oh, Henry, no, you can't…" But he pulled me onward, his arm intertwined with my own.

"My dear beautiful creature, I am the King of England and I can do as I please."

Not even the heavy headdress could shield me from their glares.

~

The next morning after terse, one of Henry's gentlemen invited me to break my fast with the king. I nodded nervously, unsure of what the king's meaning the night prior was.

When I arrived, every manner of food was spread before him in the great chamber. "Ah, my lovely sparrow…I may call you my that, may I not? Sister Elizabeth seems so formal now that we are such close friends."

"Sparrow? No, sire, I am far too strong-willed for that term of affection." Henry loved to flirt; Edmond had made that fact quite clear.

"So true. You, my lady, are surely a falcon. I shall call you my falcon, then."

I smiled as he gestured for me to sit. "Tell me, my falcon, why is that I remember Elizabeth Gregory so differently."

"Differently, sir? I hope for my sake the change is for the better."

He laughed, shoving a wedge of bread into his mouth. "She, for example, wasn't very bright at all."

"No?"

He shook his head. "As dull as a corpse."

I sipped on the wine in front of me. "Talk of corpses at our morning meal, how very grim."

"I've made a few into corpses." His warning was clear.

"So I have heard. Surely I might be far more attractive *without* a head."

He laughed loudly, his large chest heaving. "You amuse me, my falcon! Intelligent, beautiful, and now witty? It's too deadly a combination for me to bear."

"What shall we do?" I batted my eyelashes at him, exaggerating the habit of the women who vied endlessly for his attention.

"I fear we will have to spend more time getting to know you, Sister Elizabeth the Second."

EDMOND

J was out of my mind with worry. I walked the halls of the abbey, missing her so badly it ached. I'd gotten one message from Elizabeth, and reading between the lines I knew that she'd managed to get the attention of the king, and that he suspected she wasn't who she said she was. Both of these facts worried me senseless.

"Take that dog over to the orphanage," Ursula said to me in between my pacing of the hallways.

"The dog? Beast?"

She nodded. "The children adore him, diseased mongrel that he is."

"Is it possible, dear Sister of the Negative, that you have taken a shine to my fine furry friend?"

She scrunched up her face. "Such a silly notion, Father. But they could use a mood lift over there. The fever has been going around again."

"I'll see about getting a medic in. Has the sinner Lord Houston been paying his share?"

"He has, after a new round of threats."

"There's more wickedness to be confessed?"

"Oh my good father is overflowing with evil."

I whistled for Beast and listened for his large paws to slide across the stones.

"Is there any word from London? Has your beloved worked her way into the king's *special* favors yet?"

I turned my back to her, walking the behemoth dog out the door without a word.

~

"You're to be made a bishop," my uncle said to me that evening over dinner.

"Huzzah!" I said with an eye roll.

"It is a great honor, surely you are thankful."

"Beyond words," I said, stabbing my spoon into the stew. I was further entrenched into a lifestyle I deplored, and further indebted to my uncle and his causes.

"I heard from our ally, Sir Thomas More, the other day via messenger from the Palace at Whitehall."

"Is there news of Bess?"

"Yes, my lovesick boy. Your Bess has caught the eye of the king, it seems."

I nodded, my feelings quite mixed. "Is there any advancement toward our goal?"

My heart thumped in my chest waiting for his answer. I knew she was waiting for a way out of our mess; an escape plan.

"Obviously I couldn't ask More about that, now could I?"

I stared into my stew, scolding myself at the idiotic question. "No."

"No indeed. He believes that she was sent from God himself to convince Henry to set aside his plans for the divorce and return to the true faith."

We both laughed at that. "As if."

"As if, indeed," he said. "She'll convince him with her blade in his heart!"

I nervously looked around the room. All it took was for one servant to overhear, and my Elizabeth would be accused of treason. We'd *all* be accused of treason.

"She's doing well, Edmond."

I toyed with my spoon, knowing full well that he would not be pleased for long.

The very next day, I sent a trusted messenger to London. Sealed in wax with my ring, I bid her to wait. In Latin, I quoted the prophet Isaiah:

But they that wait upon the Lord shall renew their strength;
they shall mount up with wings as eagles; they shall run,
and not be weary; and they shall walk, and not faint.

ELIZABETH

I knew exactly what Edmond's handwritten message meant. Wait, keep the king close, but not too close. There had to be a way out of the impossible situation we were in.

In the meantime, I spent more and more time with Henry and grew to enjoy his company. We often played tennis, which he always beat me at, even though I'd blame the heavy robes I was forced to wear.

After one such game, he tugged at my nun's habit. "You would play far better with this off!"

"Surely Your Majesty wouldn't have naked nuns bouncing tennis balls in plain view," I teased.

"I'd have *this* fake nun bouncing all over my balls in my rooms tonight, though."

He pulled harder at my clothing, the eyes of the court watching.

"Sire! They are watching. Including your mistress!"

"Queen," he corrected.

"Mm hm," I said with the flirtatious roll of my eyes.

"Let us walk out of the view of these gossipy buzzards,

shall we?"

"As you wish." I took his powerful arm as we walked past the snickering ladies, past the stone face of Anne Boleyn, and out into the privacy of his orchards.

"You deny me as she denied me. Should I abandon the Lady Boleyn and court you, Sister?" Henry stood under the apple tree, his long arms reaching up to grasp one of the ripe fruits.

"Is that what moves you, Henry? Denial? That which you cannot have?"

"No!" he said, biting hard into the apple.

"Then what?"

"Power, love, forever. Those things move me. But, Sister Elizabeth, you *intrigue* me."

"I cannot love you." I bit into the apple he held in front of my lips.

"Ah, but you must."

"I love another." My mind drifted to my beloved Edmond.

"We *all* love another. But love is big, endless. We can love one another now, today, and continue to love them."

I allowed him to take my hand and lead me toward the rose garden. "Do you love Anne?"

"I love the woman who gives me an heir."

"That is not me."

"No. But you, my dearest one, make my heart happy at this very moment. I adore you for you, and simply that."

I smiled at him, wrapping my arm around his broad waist. "That is special indeed!"

He laughed and drew me near, and as we walked amongst the vibrant roses, I felt the joy of being in that moment. For a few luscious minutes, I forgot about the cares of the shadow that hung over us all.

∼

Later the next day, I experienced the other side of the king: the bratty, spoiled side that Edmond had warned me about. "Steer clear of angering him, Bess," he'd said countless times while we were at the abbey.

But we'd gotten too close, and one rainy afternoon, it all unraveled. It happened while we were discussing literature and scripture. I'd argued with him, questioning his interpretation of a line in a text we were poring over. His eyes lit up when I'd engaged him. Instead of drawing his anger, I drew his admiration.

"You dare disagree with your monarch?" he'd bellowed in fake outrage.

"No, sire, I'm simply saying that I think Saint Augustine meant…"

"A woman who argues with a man," he teased.

"A nun, that has to count for something, Your Majesty?" I'd teased back.

He leaned in close, our faces nearly touching. "You are no more a nun than I am a virgin!"

I laughed. For the first time since I'd left Edmond's side, I truly laughed.

And, when his stout arms wrapped around my narrow waist, I liked it. Desire rose in me, and with that, guilt. So I ran.

And ran.

I ran across the fields, over the creek, and through the veil of the autumn showers with Henry steps behind me. His legs were long, but I was lighter and faster.

Eventually, however, his long stride overcame mine, and he caught up with me.

"I-I'm sorry. I don't know what came over me," I whimpered when he finally pulled me into the shelter of the hedges. But the truth was I knew exactly what had me upset; I'd almost kissed him. *I wanted to kiss him!*

"Elizabeth, please do not be afraid of me. Never will I harm you."

"I fear that is not the complete truth."

We sat on a stone bench under the boughs of a tree. After a long silence, he asked the question I feared he would. "Who has your heart?"

"Father Gregory."

"Of course!" A wave of recognition washed over him. "Of course."

"Do not tell anyone, please, Henry."

His broad hand took mine and squeezed it. "It shall be our secret."

We sat in silence, his hand around mine, watching the mist of rain.

"Elizabeth, why can we not share more? I'm not asking for you to love me, I'm simply asking you to let what is brewing between us breathe."

"Such lovely words for a man attempting to get into a woman's skirts," I said, leaning into him.

"It's more than that. I'm drawn to you; I have been from the first time our eyes met. No, you cannot be my love, and I can never truly have you. But what's the harm in two friends comforting each other for a season?"

"Why do you need comfort, Your Majesty?"

"Everything is out of hand. It wasn't that I didn't love Catherine."

"Queen Catherine?"

"She is no longer queen!"

"And Anne will be?"

"When she bears me a son, as she has promised. Until then, I shall not crown her."

"So you left Catherine simply because you thought Anne could give you an heir?

He shook his head. "Not entirely. My desire for Catherine

had long since cooled when I was beguiled by the Boleyn sisters."

"And your Catherine is past the age of motherhood?" I asked.

"Yes," he nodded. "But it isn't simply that, as I'm accused. The marriage to Catherine was never valid; it was sinful."

"Because she was your brother's widow?"

"Yes."

I looked into his eyes, and saw that he believed what he said. "There was dispensation from the pope. And, of course, their marriage was never consummated."

"Lies." He waved his hand in the air, as if brushing away the falsity. "They were in love, and she was wedded and bedded in every way."

"She told you?" I was astounded. The entire nation believed the myth of a virginal Catherine of Aragon being wedded to the young Prince Henry. Now, sitting there with the larger-than-life king, I realized how naïve I truly had been.

"She didn't have to. I *saw* them. More than once." He shot me a wink. "I like to watch."

"Oh!" I said, taking it all in. "But, sire," I said. "If memory serves me, the papal dispensation made allowances for that indiscreet bit of detail, did it not?"

He nodded. "Yes, but Leviticus does not! It was sin, and because of that sin, we were denied an heir."

I searched my mind for the scripture he was referring to. "Does it not say something along the lines of, 'If a man shall take his brother's wife, it is an impurity; he hath uncovered his brother's nakedness; they shall be childless.'"

"Yes. Do you see why I have no choice?"

"No," I admitted. "You *have* a child with Catherine, the Princess Mary."

"The Lady Mary," he grumbled. "And she is not a son!"

He was getting agitated, and I had no desire to fuel his already-mercurial mood. "So Anne, then, you feel is your rightful wife. But you do not love her? Surely you could have chosen any woman you wished?"

"Not any, but I did love her. Or I thought I did. I think what I really loved was the chase. But it is far too late to turn back now. My path is with Anne, whether it makes me miserable or not."

"So your misery is of your own doing."

"And yours, dear Elizabeth, is also my doing." His eyes softened, and the stroke of his finger on the top of my hand intensified.

I nodded, my eyes looking into his. I saw an opportunity, a way to get Edmond back. "Oh please, Henry, allow Edmond at court. I'd do anything."

"Anything?" His hand slid to my thigh.

Before I could answer, he withdrew it. "Not that way," he sighed. "I want you, and I'm determined to have you, but not that way."

"So he can return to court? You were friends once, he told me."

"Did he tell you what came between us?"

I shook my head.

He bit his lip and tilted his head, as if weighing whether he should answer my unspoken question. "Catherine," was all he said.

I was left puzzled as he pulled me to my feet and we walked arm in arm back to the palace.

~

The dark eyes of Anne Boleyn were waiting for us as we ducked into the courtyard, laughing and shaking off the rain.

"Henry, we need to speak," she snapped.

I tried to pull my arm away, but he held it tight. Even worse, his hand stroked the top of mine, a clear affront to her in the presence of her ladies.

"Sire, I shall go. They will be needing me to set up for matins." I once again tried to withdraw, but the king held my arm even tighter.

"We shall retire to my chambers for a private mass, Sister."

Arm in arm, we turned toward the door.

"Ladies, we shall join the king, my husband, for services," Anne said with a clap of her hands to her ladies.

"Oh no, Sister Elizabeth and I shall be very much alone," he snapped, never turning around.

When we arrived in his private apartments, I turned on him. I was furious; and despite the voice inside me screaming to stay calm. I railed at him. Even worse, I did it in front of his gentlemen of the chamber.

"How could you?" I howled.

"Calm, Sister. This level of anger may not be good for your health!"

"You put a target on my head! That snake wants to see me fall!"

"That snake is carrying my child! Hold your tongue."

And I should have. But I didn't. "Send me to the Tower then Henry! You may as well. You've just doomed me!"

He fell into his massive chair, his face red. "Oh, you may well end up in the Tower! But not yet. Get to your rooms, and do not let me see your face again until I call for you."

Henry's closest servants tried to pull me from his presence, but I resisted. I was determined to finish the argument out, stubborn fool that I was. Fearing for me, they lifted me up and in a fit of drama, carried me through the air from his apartments and down the hall.

Henry's best friend, Sir Charles Brandon, the Duke of

Suffolk, stopped them in the midst of the great hall. "Sister, can I help you?" His face was painted with the devious grin he was known for.

They set me down in front of him.

He offered his arm and dismissed the laughing group of young men. "Say nothing of this!" he called out to their backs.

When we arrived at my chamber door, he asked, "What happened?"

"I might have screamed at the king. In front of everyone."

He laughed. "He does like fiery women."

"I should go apologize."

"Let him calm down and call for you. I shall assure him that you are much repentant."

"Thank you," I said.

Before leaving, he leaned down and whispered in my ear. "I like fiery women, too, *Sister* Elizabeth. If you should ever need any further diversion, send word to me."

"Yes, Your Grace," I murmured, pulling away from him. Brandon was handsome and charming, but further entanglements were the *last* thing I needed.

～

The next few days were nerve-wracking. Constantly looking over my shoulder, waiting to be arrested or worse, I wondered how angry Henry truly was. It was no secret that he changed moods, and allegiances, quite quickly and falling out with him could prove dangerous, even deadly.

Even though there was no word from Henry, I was soothed by a letter from Edmond. Although his seal was broken, meaning the message had been read, his meaning was clear. He quoted Luke 21:28 in Latin:

His autem fieri incipientibus respicite et levate capita vestra quoniam adpropinquat redemptio vestra.

Which I quickly translated to:

But when these things begin to happen, look up, and lift up your heads; for your redemption draweth nigh.

Edmond was telling me to wait a little longer; he had found a way out.

~

It was two more long days before Henry called for me. Sir Charles Brandon himself knocked on my door. "The king would like to speak with you," he said.

Be brave, I told myself, willing my knees not to wobble.

"Is he still angry?" I asked.

"With Harry, who knows?" He shrugged and offered his arm, walking me through the long halls to the king's chambers.

"Ah, what a lovely sight! Sister, please, sit," Henry said with the wave of his hand toward the chair, as if nothing had happened.

"Shall I stay?" Brandon asked with a lascivious glance toward me.

"Hm, I would share, Charles, but this one has not warmed to me yet!" He laughed, the contagious belly laugh of a happy Henry.

We all laughed, relieved that the king was in a good mood, finally.

"Surely none could deny *you*, Your Majesty?" Brandon said with a wink.

"Ah, Charles, I think her heart belongs to that heart-breaker Gregory."

"Sir Edmond Gregory," Brandon said with a whistle. "Forgive him, Harry, and we could *all* have some fun!"

"Out, out," Henry shouted with another burst of laughter.

I waited for him to speak, but he did not. On his second glass of wine, my own glass remaining empty, I broke protocol and spoke.

"Henry, Your Majesty, I do apologize for my temper. I am new to court and found myself overwhelmed with my affection for—"

He waved his hand in the air, silencing me. "Oh stop, please. Who told you to speak like that? Forget courtly manners and just say it!"

"I *am* sorry. A hot temper is one of my flaws."

"It's one of your greatest assets! I do love a good verbal joust!" He smiled, his blue eyes sparkling in the candlelight. "You are forgiven. And we," he said, placing his hand on his chest, "will endeavor to be more patient with our fair Sister Elizabeth."

"Thank you, sire."

He reached toward the flask and filled my glass. "Now, let's drink and continue our conversation about Leviticus, shall we?"

"As you wish."

"Or," he said, leaning in close, his deep voice nearly a whisper. "Or, perhaps you'd rather discuss Luke 21:28?"

I merely shrugged, not at all surprised that Henry had been reading my correspondence from Edmond.

BISHOP EDMOND GREGORY

*M*y uncle, the new cardinal, paced across the floor, his face as red as the robes he now wore.

"Rome is *not* pleased," he finally hissed, turning on his heel to make another trip across the uneven floorboards.

"Shocking, Your Eminence."

He turned on me, his lips curled in a sneer. "Careful, my nephew. Even I won't be able to protect your little lover if something doesn't happen quickly."

With a gulp, I thought of my dear Elizabeth. She was entrenched in no man's land between the throne of England and the Pope of Rome. And here I sat, drinking wine and doing nothing.

Interrupting my thoughts, he hurled his venom at me again. "How has she not managed to be alone with the most lascivious monarch in the world?"

"It's a large court, and a nun can't exactly saunter into the king's rooms, now can she?"

He collapsed into his stuffed chair, and with a defeated

sigh admitted, "I know, but Sir Thomas said the king fancied her. If she could just get closer to him, get him alone..."

"The King of England is rarely alone."

"She knows too much, Edmond. If she fails, I fear we will have to..."

"Don't!" I howled, hopping to my feet like a wild rabbit.

"I like the girl, and you know my affection for you. You are the son I never had."

A son you'll strangle when he no longer suits you, I thought.

"I'm going to court," I finally said. "There is no other option."

"You? Do you forget that our dear monarch banned you from court years ago? Are you really willing to lose your head for this mission?"

"No," I answered truthfully. "But I'd do anything for Elizabeth."

"Including bed Jolly King Harry?" he asked.

"Including that. Especially that," I said with a grin, remembering those long summer nights at Richmond Palace when we were little more than teens.

"Blasphemy," he said with a laugh, finally relaxing.

"Sodomy, buggery, treason – all in a day's work for a lowly priest."

"*Bishop*, you mean. Get this done, and you'll wear red cardinal robes alongside me, I swear it."

I shook my head. "I want *her*. My dream is to leave all of this and take Elizabeth someplace where we can quietly live as man and wife."

My uncle stood and looked at me with pity. "This you must do, but you will never be free of the will of the church."

"Do you promise to get us out and to safety if this thing is done soon?"

"Of course," he lied.

"Both of us."

"Certainly," he said, as if he'd ever planned to protect my Elizabeth.

ELIZABETH

*H*is fingers wrapped around my throat, and the warmth of his breath was on my cheek. "I must have you *now*."

My hand left the blade hidden in my skirts as the sound of his voice washed over me. "My love!" I squealed.

"Shh, darling, we must remain hidden." His lips fell hard against mine, the hardness under his robes pressing into my body.

"You're here; you came," I said into his deep kisses.

"I *am* here, and I'm about to come." His tongue found mine, and we entangled into the needy kiss of two lovers long parted.

"It's been so long," I panted, clawing at his layers of priestly clothing. When I had his member freed, I grasped it with my hand. He moaned, far too loudly for our safety. "Oh my love," I said, my lips finding his again.

His strong arms lifted me as I wrapped my legs around his waist. "I'll surely perish if we are not one this second," I begged.

"I've dreamt of this moment when I'd be inside you again," he said in my ear, plunging deep inside me.

As he thrust, a loud moan escaped my lips, his own mouth falling on mine, silencing my ecstasy lest we be discovered.

My entire being erupted as he spilled deep inside of me, my legs straining to hold on to him.

Minutes later, tangled up in each other, we fell to the cold floor.

"I love you. You are mine, and I am yours, always," he whispered as we fell asleep.

EDMOND

*D*eep in the night, I felt the gentle nudge of a foot in my naked ribs. I sat up with a start, seeking my robe in the near-darkness. *We'd been discovered!*

"Fear not, Father, it is I," she said, the contempt in her voice unmistakable.

"Ursula, what are you doing here?" I pulled my robe over my nakedness, away from her candlelight, away from her prying eyes.

"Your sister sent me to watch over you. Clearly she was right!"

"Go," I said, pointing toward the open doorway.

"As you wish, but I shan't leave court until Joan the Abbess commands me to."

She left like a whirlwind, not bothering to close the door behind her.

"Ursula," Elizabeth moaned from behind me.

"Indeed. We must keep her close."

"I hate that wench! And she hates us. I'm tempted to wring her scrawny neck as if she were to be my Sunday roast."

I chuckled. "Dear Elizabeth, you must learn to keep your enemies close. Never underestimate the power of hatred. Love is stronger, but hatred must be respected."

"I guess," she said, slipping her heavy robes over her head.

When we were dressed, I once again pulled her close. My nose touched hers, and I inhaled her scent. "I must go, but tomorrow night I shall see the king."

"I've resisted him thus far, but I'm getting closer. Do you want me to arrange an audience?"

I shook my head and took her lovely face into my hands. "Do nothing for now, for I have a plan. We'll talk soon and I'll explain, but for now we need to prepare for prime."

~

"Edmond," the king said tersely the very next day. We hadn't spoken in years.

"Your Majesty, thank you for seeing me and allowing me to express my supplication for our past disagreements, I—"

"Let's dispense with formalities. I've had your cock in my mouth, after all."

"And I yours," I said, his frankness shocking even me. "Harry, I am truly sorry that we quarreled, I've missed you."

"Not enough," he growled, slumping back into his chair.

"You did ban me from court."

"You kept your head, Father. That should tell you something."

"*Father*...I'd rather not be *Father*."

"Your Grace, then. You are welcome back to court. But why are you here? After all these years?"

I searched my mind for an answer, but eventually settled on the truth. "To protect you."

"Wine," he commanded with a snap of his fingers. Several young pages jumped to serve the king.

"Sit, Edmond, my old friend."

I sat across from him; hopeful I wasn't about to be thrown into the Tower, or worse.

Our eyes met over the heavy cups. Despite age and the toll of stress, he was the same Harry I knew. He'd been my closest friend, my hunting partner, and my constant companion until his brother died. After that, it all changed. I was sent home from court by his father, the shrewd King Henry the Seventh.

Once a second son, destined to the clergy the same as me, we'd studied together. After Arthur's untimely death in Wales, Henry had been whisked away to be kept safe by his mourning parents. Going from a spare to the heir had altered the course of his life.

After his father's death, I'd been foolish enough to oppose his marriage to his former sister-in-law. Harry had always been rash, and with the stroke of a pen I was banished from his life. Until now.

"You might have been right about Catherine," he said, refilling our cups with his own hand. He shooed away the servants with two words. "Leave us."

When the room was cleared, I pressed the matter.

"My outspokenness nearly cost me my life."

"I would have never done that. I was angry, but my love for you merely needed you to be away from us until my temper cooled."

"What's changed?" I asked, as if I didn't already know. The king had grown tired of his much-older, now barren wife. The younger Anne bore the promise of sons, which he desperately needed. One daughter was not going to secure his throne.

"What's changed? Everything."

"Ah, you're in love! Or is this truly about sons?"

"Now? It's about an heir. The love I once felt for Anne has

cooled. She says, though, that she may with child."

"And the pope will not grant a divorce from Catherine?"

He shook his head. "No, but I may not need him for long. It's time for me to become head of my own church. I refuse to answer to Rome much longer."

I leaned back in my chair, sensing the world was about to change forever. "I can say no more, but my uncle is opposed. He will stop at nothing to preserve the Mother Church."

"Anyone one who opposes me is in far graver danger than I," he warned.

I gulped down the wine and refilled my own cup without his bidding. He stood up and walked across the room.

"Come closer, dear friend, and tell me of this beautiful imposter I crave." He patted the velvet coverlet of his massive bed for me to sit.

"My cousin, Sister Elizabeth?"

He laughed, his strong arm wrapping around my leaner frame. "That's not Elizabeth. She is an imposter."

"People change over time, Majesty."

He raised his large hand to me. "It's better for your health if you remain silent rather than lie to me. I've knew your cousin Elizabeth quite well, and she had a thin scar alongside the back of her ear. This woman, although a work of art, does not."

I decided to go with silence.

"Should I ask where the real sweet Cousin Elizabeth is?"

"No, Majesty."

~

It was twenty-four hours before I could be alone with her again. Twenty-four long, grueling hours. By the time I was in her bed, my entire being shook with need for her.

"What a long day!" she said, lying back on her silken pillows.

"The king sent bedding?"

She glanced guiltily at the fine linens adorning her luxurious bed. It was certainly not the standard bedding for a nun, even one of noble birth.

"He did," she said slowly.

"Has he been in the bed?"

"No!" She flung herself to my chest.

"My love, the king will have you. He must, if he wants you. He is the king, after all."

Her face was stained with tears when she looked up at me. "I feel so guilty even engaging him in this way! The linens, the evenings with the fine wine, all of it makes me feel untrue to you."

I dried her tears with my fingertips. "Sweet Bess, I'm not sure how to begin…"

When she was calm, her luscious body against my own, I decided to test the waters.

"Henry and I were close. *Quite* close…"

"Of course," she said, nuzzling into my chest. "Like brothers."

She yawned, and I decided that the sticky conversation I'd been avoiding could wait.

"Not exactly. Back then, when we were lads studying under the same tutor, Prince Harry and I were inseparable."

"What happened?"

"After his father died, he took the throne. And, much to my heartbreak, decided to marry his brother's widow, Catherine of Aragon."

"He had to."

"He did not!"

"Edmond, he needed an heir. The Tudors had to have a

male heir! Even an uneducated peasant like myself knew that."

I stroked her hair. I often forgot how young she was; how simple her early years were. "I wasn't angry that he married her. I was angry that he loved her."

"I don't understand," she said, pulling me close.

"I know, my darling. In time, it will all be clearer. But for now, we need to keep Henry close."

"Edmond, perhaps I should proceed with the murder I've been charged with? If the pope has promised his help?"

"Rome is a bigger bed of snakes than the Tudor court. No, we will trust neither side in this unholy war."

"Then we are stuck!"

I nestled into her, content to have her close, at least for the moment. "I have a plan, my love," I reassured her. "At the moment, Henry is far more powerful than both my uncle and maybe even Rome. If we can unite in some sort of bond with him, I believe we can all be free."

"And then we'll finally all be happy?"

"We will, my love, I promise. Henry will never be happy."

"Why?" she asked.

"Because he is never content with what he has."

~

I didn't mean for it to happen, but it did.

I'd managed to get a message to Henry to meet me in the crypt. It was the only place I could think of to be truly alone. Other than our chambers in the dead of the night, the crypt had quickly become the only place that Elizabeth and I met in private during the long days at the palace.

A rumor had recently went around court that the crypt was haunted, and that several disgruntled royals buried there were displeased over the treatment of Queen Catherine.

They were rising up and were very dangerous. Of course, I started this rumor.

And for a king to be hanging around a haunted burial ground deep underneath the chapel royal was so unthinkable that I knew we would be completely alone. My goal that afternoon was to convince him that we were on his side, but he needed to help us. Instead, the snugness of the area that afternoon got the better of my self-control.

I didn't mean to, but that afternoon in the quiet of the crypt, I shared a kiss with Henry. It was quick, chaste, and bore none of the passion of our youth, but it opened the floodgate between us that never truly went away.

"Edmond, please," he said. "Just a little more."

It wasn't that the fire didn't still burn in me for him. I'd always love him, but my bond was to my Elizabeth. "Harry, I can't—"

"One more," he breathed, leaning into me to brush his lips against my own.

And then it happened.

From the corner of my eye, I saw my beloved watching in the shadows.

"Bess!" I screamed to her back as she ran from the dark crypt. "Bess, please, wait!"

I chased after her, leaving Henry bewildered behind us. He wasn't in the habit of answering to anyone, especially not a woman.

After an hour of combing the many public rooms and the expansive lawn, I finally found her deep in the garden at dusk. I expected tears, but I should have known better. Elizabeth stared at me, her gaze as stone as the gargoyles leering down at us.

"How could you!"

"We're old friends, my love, what you saw was just courtly…"

"What I saw was you kissing someone else as you might me."

"You are mistaken," I lied. "You're still young and innocent and you misread…"

She grabbed a handful of roses, the thorns causing blood to run from her precious palms. My bold Bess didn't flinch.

"Liar!" she howled, smacking me in the face with the handful of roses.

As the petals fell across my robes and to the ground, I let the truth spill from my rose-scented lips. "Alright, Alright. I shall tell you everything. Please, in private. If we are seen thus, my darling, we will be undone."

"Tell me now before I strangle you."

"Bess…"

"Don't *Bess* me! You *kissed* the king! The king we're tasked with killing, I might add."

"Shh," I warned. "Don't *ever* say that out loud!"

I tried to take her hand, but she jerked away from me like an eel.

"Please, Elizabeth. Let's sit. I'll explain everything."

I managed to get her to follow me to a marble bench hidden in the heavy shrubbery. "First, I loved him once. In the way a man loves a woman. Well, not exactly like that, but we were lovers."

"How long ago?"

"It was years ago. Do you remember my story of my first love, the royal kiss?"

She nodded, waves of realization washing over her. "It is such a new world for me to fathom."

"I know, my darling. I'm sorry. But the world is gigantic; love is endless. There's not a box that it fits into, despite what the church would have you believe."

"And sin is…?"

"A lie created by those in power to control the masses."

152

"Where does all of this leave us?" she asked.

"I love you, Bess. You're my everything, my forever. But my love for others doesn't just die because of that."

"Do you love him now?" Her eyes were hard, ominous.

"Not as I love you. But a part of me will always love the Harry I shared my youth with." She glared at me, but her fingers dropped the weapon of roses to the ground.

"You shouldn't have kissed," she said, her tone softening.

"No, I shouldn't have kissed him *without your permission*."

"Oh," she said, clearly intrigued by this new concept. "And, Edmond, I have this power? Of *permission*?"

I knew I had her. My love's mind was brilliant, and open. And perhaps, just perhaps, this new concept wouldn't tear us apart after all.

"A man, asking a woman. That is a new idea to me." Her hand reached out for mine, the pain of the thorns of the roses forgotten for the moment.

"My dear Bess, you have power over me, over men, that you have not even begun to grasp. You are my true love, and although I confess he was my first love, I shall not touch him again unless you want me to."

She leaned into me. "So many revelations! I will think on this, Father Gregory."

"Bishop Gregory now," I corrected, sneaking a kiss.

ELIZABETH

The very next day after mass, Edmond pulled me aside. "It's Ursula," he said in my ear.

"It's always Ursula," I groaned. "What now?"

"My sister didn't send her. This morning I received a message from Joan; it seems Sister Ursula fled the convent without permission."

"Oh my!"

"Yes," he nodded. "Of course Joan is brokenhearted. She sees this as an *emotional* matter, shall we say."

"Could it be?" I asked.

He shook his head. "And she'd come *here*? Unbidden?"

I searched my mind for an answer. "If not Joan, then maybe your uncle sent her here? To watch us?"

"Maybe," he whispered. "But he hates her, too."

"We'll talk tonight. I have to get down to the palace gates to give out alms."

"Bess, you can't. What if someone sees you?"

"In London? Who on earth would recognize me in London? That's a world away from Worthington."

"I know, but is it worth the risk?"

"Edmond, two things are keeping me sane right now. You and my hours spent feeding the destitute of this city in need."

"Be careful, please? We'll talk of Ursula more later."

I nodded, gathering up my basket of bread. "In bed?"

"Always," he said with a risky pat of my bottom.

Later that night, Edmond was once again hidden in my chambers thanks to the privacy afforded us by the king himself. I whispered into his ear, "It's Wolsey."

"You're in love with old wrinkled up Cardinal Wolsey?" he teased.

"I suspect Ursula is reporting to him. I saw them whispering during vespers."

"That is odd. I can't imagine them exactly being friends, can you?"

"No," I agreed. "A plot is brewing."

"We have to find out what she's up to," he said.

"The king would know who arranged her assignment here."

"Yes," he agreed. "But if she's told Wolsey of our plot, we have trouble on the way."

"I could take care of Wolsey."

"I'm not sure we're on opposite sides, exactly. He has his eyes on the papacy with the same desire as my uncle. I think his focus is on satisfying the king as far as giving him Anne. I'm not sure he wants to see England split from Rome."

"But if Henry breaks from the church, everything is up in the air."

"I don't think Cardinal Wolsey wants that," he said.

"But Anne does, and she's convinced Henry."

"Yes," Edmond said. "But for now, we have time for one more romp in this fine bed before we must get some rest."

"Always eager," I teased.

"For you, every second of every day."

~

It took a few days for me to be alone with Henry again. Late one evening, one of his gentlemen came to my door to bid me to take a cup of ale with the king. I glanced to Edmond, naked and hiding behind a wardrobe. With a nod, he gave me his unspoken approval to do what was needed.

When I arrived in his sleeping chamber, Henry was dressed in his sleeping clothes. "Surely, Your Majesty, you haven't bid me here to bed?"

"I wish," he sighed. "But your love has proved most elusive."

I walked forward, glancing back as the door was closed behind me. I'd never been alone with him near a bed before. "Your Majesty, should we involve Edmond in this conversation?"

"No, no, I plan to behave. I promised you that I would. Sit, my falcon."

We sat in the velvet chairs in front of the fire, sipping warm ale as the night grew late. "I wanted to apologize for what you saw in the crypt the other day. It was my doing," he said.

"I was caught of guard, Henry. I've since gained a greater understanding of such things."

"Good, good. Because the truth is, dear Elizabeth, I want to kiss him again. Everywhere. And I want to kiss you, too. My desire for you both is like an inferno, it seems."

"And your wife?"

He sighed. "I have to force myself to touch Anne."

"Your other wife, I meant."

He took a long sip of the ale. "Like a dog with a bone, aren't you my lovely? Let this go."

"Yes, sire."

He pulled his chair closer to mine. "Since you like to talk

of Catherine, has Edmond told you what tore us apart? Why he was banned from my presence?"

"He said that he didn't approve of your marriage to her. For the same reason you said, I assume. Affinity, as she was your brother's wife."

Henry slammed his great fist on the wooden arm of the chair. "Edmond doesn't give a rat's arse about cannon law. No, he was jealous."

"He didn't want to lose you, I suppose."

"Unreasonable! I was the King of England – I *had* to marry."

"Yes," I agreed. "And so Edmond had to go."

"No, no, that was never the plan. His own jealousy is the reason we were torn apart. Catherine loved him too! My Spanish queen was more than willing to let us share our love by three, in secret. Edmond refused."

"So you banned him?"

"No, I banned him because he dared speak out from the pulpit in Cambridge in opposition of my marriage!"

"Oh," I said. As shocking as it was, I could completely imagine Edmond doing such a thing.

"But now, I am willing to let that rift be mended. The affection I bear for you both is what sustains me in this nest of wasps."

"We can't stay, Henry. You know that."

"But you must! I need you."

I shook my head. "That nest of wasps is plotting against us as we speak. They will stop at nothing to bring us down. It will happen, and soon."

"Our time is limited then." He refilled our cups as we stared into the crackling fire.

"Henry, can I ask you something?"

"I'll answer anything if you kiss me. Just once, I must know what it feels like for our lips to meet."

I leaned into him, the guilt now gone as our lips met.

After I pulled away from him, not wanting the night to go any further without Edmond, he leaned back into his chair. "That was magic," he said.

"My question is who sent for Sister Ursula Houston?"

"She was requested personally by the queen."

"Catherine?"

"Anne!" he bellowed, rising to his feet.

I stood, and with a curtsey said, "Goodnight, my dear Henry. Let's continue this kiss later, perhaps with our Edmond?"

He smiled. "Come hunting with me tomorrow, my falcon. Bring Father Gregory with you. The stags are quite rampant this time of year."

"I bet they are," I said with a salacious grin.

~

The next morning, I met Edmond in the crypt. "You did well, Bess. We just need him a little closer, and then we shall use him to untangle us from this dark situation."

"Are we just using him?" My face fell.

"No, my darling. Our affection is genuine, is it not?" he asked.

"I don't love him as you do, but my affection for him I find to be growing in a way I did not expect."

Edmond smiled at me. "Elizabeth, it has to be all of us. My soul is bound with yours, no matter my history with Henry. I shall never touch him again unless it be at your bidding."

"Oh Edmond! I've given you my permission, as long as you love me."

"My love for you is eternal. But it's not simply your permission I seek, my love. I want your participation."

"And if I do not wish that?"

"Then we shall leave this place and the king behind without ever knowing that particular pleasure."

My palms grew sweaty at the word pleasure. At the thought of pleasure. With Edmond, our nights were heavenly, sensuous, truly perfect. But I couldn't deny that the idea of engaging with both men quickened my pulse.

"Possibly." I leaned into him. "But only with you, only together. Promise me?"

"I swear it," he said, his lips finding mine.

~

The next afternoon in the midst of the deer hunt, the three of us lay across the massive feather-stuffed bed in the hunting lodge. "They know we're in here," I worried.

"Of course they do. I am seeking your spiritual guidance," he said with a naughty grin. "Tell me, Sister, will my soul be eternally damned if I do *this*?" Henry's large hand worked its way into Edmond's trousers.

My eyes went to Edmond's swelling member. "I think, as a mere lowly woman, that you *might* be a sinner, Majesty."

He smiled at me, his blue eyes dancing at the dangerous game. "There's nothing lowly about you, Sister Elizabeth."

His agile fingers freed Edmond from the captivity of his garments, leaving his naked skin exposed. "But you aren't really a nun," Henry said, licking his lips at the sight of Edmond's hardness.

"No, sire," I admitted.

"Well, then, perhaps you should also partake of His Eminence alongside me?"

"If it would please you, Father?"

Edmond moaned in anticipation, his head falling back onto the silk pillow. "Stop teasing me," he begged. The waves of his dark hair cascaded over the pillow. He was beautiful that afternoon, tortured by the lust for the two people he wanted most in the world.

"I love you," I said. My lips lowered to his, my tongue stroking his.

His fist wrapped in my hair, pulling me close as my mouth devoured him.

Beneath me, Edmond's hips bucked up as Henry freed him of the cumbersome trousers. He moaned into my kiss.

"May I kiss him lower, my falcon?"

I pulled away from Edmond's hungry lips. "Does a king need to ask?"

"Ah," Henry said, his hand on my hip. He drew closer, his lips at the back of my neck. "He is no longer mine. My lovely Edmond belongs to you. But, I would taste him one more time if it did not displease you."

Edmond pulled me closer to him, craving my mouth again. "Yes, Henry, take him thus!" I could bear no more separation as my tongue stroked at Edmond's. Beneath us, I could hear the sound of Henry suckling my Edmond, driving him nearly to ecstasy.

"Ah," Edmond moaned. "Not yet."

"More? You want more?" Henry asked.

"It is now *I* who would like to share," Edmond said. A gave him a nod of agreement as he lifted my heavy skirts and exposed my nakedness to the king.

"Can this delicate bird handle two?" Henry flirted.

I reached back and pulled him close, positioning him behind me. "I'm a falcon, and will wear you *both* out," I said. With a moan of pleasure, my teeth sank into Edmond's neck as both men thrust deep within me.

~

That afternoon in the hunting lodge, we forgot that the outside world was always watching, always plotting. Throughout the afternoon, we engaged in pleasures I'd never imagined.

As the sun moved lower in the sky, we knew it was time to leave our private sanctuary. "That was careless," Edmond said, finishing his wine in front of the fire.

"But oh so good," the king said with a lusty grin.

"So good," I repeated, licking my bruised lips. Everything ached, but my entire being was racked with the aftershocks of our lovemaking.

"Henry, you know how dangerous it is, even for a king."

He nodded. "Yes, sodomy is a hard accusation even for me to escape from. Perhaps someday, when I form my church, I can change things."

Edmond stood up and damped out our fire. "Someday, but not for centuries I predict. But perhaps, in the far future, people shall be free to love as they wish."

"But as for now, I must be free to marry whom I please. Can you not see that Edmond?"

"Breaking with Rome is dangerous. Go back to Catherine; name an heir. Let this arrogant plan for a Church of England die."

"I cannot, my dearest Edmond. I fear the plot is already in motion."

Edmond looked to me. We both knew the perilous position we were in, and if Henry could be convinced to return to Rome, we might be free. But the stubborn king was steadfast, and that afternoon we knew it.

EDMOND

She sat across from me in the confessional booth. I wasn't sure why. Although not yet queen, Anne Boleyn lived as one and had her own confessor.

"Are you here to unburden your soul, my lady?"

She chuckled and leaned into the screen. "My soul is quite burdened, Bishop Gregory. Quite burdened indeed."

"Please then, confess your sins and unburden yourself."

Her lips were inches from mine; her dark eyes hooded under her heavy eyelashes. She wasn't beautiful, but she was intriguing. And she was far too intelligent to play with.

"It seems my husband, the king, has been engaging in an adulterous affair."

"I didn't realize you were married?"

Her eyes blazed with anger. "We may as well be!"

"May as well be is not the same as receiving the sacrament of marriage, or even betrothal."

Her small hand smacked the iron screen that divided us. "Enough, Father! This game you are playing is deadly."

"Deadly for whom, my lady?"

"You'd be wise to refer to me as your queen, for that is

what I am. At this moment, I am carrying the heir to the Tudor throne in my very womb. I can't bring myself to do harm to an ordained priest, even a blasphemous one, but there is no such protection for one pretending to be a nun."

I sat back on the bench, shielding myself from her. "Pretending?"

"Henry told me when she arrived at court that first day that it was not your cousin Elizabeth after all. He knows she's a fake! It's only a matter of time until he tires of you, and when he does, her head will roll."

"My lady, I have no idea of what you speak."

"You shall call me Your Majesty!" She smacked the screen again in defiance.

"Never."

"I *heard* the three of you, Father. The *three* of you! Sinning in the hunting lodge."

As if kicked in the gut, her words hit me. I knew we'd been brazen in our affections the day prior, and now Anne knew. Our carelessness had given her power.

"Tell me, *Anne*, does he love you as he does me? Or has he grown tired of you already?"

The door to the wooden booth slammed as she stormed out of the chapel.

～

"Our situation has become dire, my love."

Elizabeth looked at me and nodded. I saw no fear in her eyes. "Yes," she agreed.

"Henry confirmed that Ursula was brought by Anne Boleyn?"

"Yes again," she answered.

"Ursula has never approved of you, but I oddly felt she

cared for me. I'm going to stop the whispers and speak directly with her."

"Be careful," Elizabeth said. "She could be the devil herself."

I tilted my head, thinking. "I don't think so, Bess. I saw her at that orphanage. Did you know she begged me to let Beast stay with the children? They love him."

"Beast! I so wish he could be here."

"I miss him, but he belongs there. He roams the halls at night, protecting the orphans. They need him more than we do."

"He was born to serve."

I nodded. "Yes, and that was Ursula's doing. She's broken, seriously broken, but I don't believe all is lost with her just yet."

"And Joan loves her," Elizabeth said. "So for Joan, we have to try."

~

It was easy to switch schedules with Father Barza the next day. Ursula was a creature of habit, and always went to the confession booth at the same time every day. So, the next morning, after ten boring confessions, I had her where I wanted her.

"Forgive me Father, for I have sinned," she began, her tone matter-of-fact as usual.

"Yes, you have, my Sister. In fact, you've sinned against *my* sister, haven't you?"

I expected a fight, but what I got instead was unexpected. Tears. Slumped into a ball, her body shook from her sobs.

"Is it true? Was I right, then?"

More sniffles, but no words came from the other side of the screen. "Do you indeed have a heart? A conscience?"

"I never meant for it to go this far! I swear Edmond, I never wanted you to be in harm's way."

"But Elizabeth?"

"At first, I hated her. She was free; free to be dead. Free to seek vengeance, free to love. Freer than I will ever be. But now, I would never hurt her. I've come to see that you're a decent person. And I never would cause Joan pain."

"You left her, though. In the night, no less. She's written to me endlessly of her heartbreak."

"I had no choice! Don't you understand? I could not let *her*…do what it is she came to do."

"Our goals have changed. At this point, both sides can burn in hell. We just want out."

I heard her take a deep breath. "Anne Boleyn called for me. I've been a secret supporter of the protestant movement from the beginning."

"Why?"

"I hate the church that suppresses me, and those like me. You of all people should understand."

"I understand that the protestant movement will be no less oppressive than the Catholic Church. If you expect reform to that degree, you are delusional."

"So you sit there a bishop, and don't believe in anything."

"I've had no choice. You, however, are choosing to insert yourself into this great war."

"You don't think Henry can split peacefully? Make England a better place?"

"No, I don't. There won't be peace, and Henry as head of any church is a terrifying prospect."

"No worse than the current pope!"

"True," I conceded. "But I'm fighting for Elizabeth."

"And Henry?"

"I'd love to see him prosper."

"And live?"

"Long live the king," I said.

"Anne thinks that Elizabeth is here to seduce the king, to draw him from her and back to the true faith."

I laughed, although the idea wasn't preposterous. We'd definitely attempted to use our affections to sway the king. "Go home, Ursula."

"I can't! They've threatened to reveal my relationship with Joan. They have evidence, letters. Very intimate letters…"

I took a deep breath. "This court does love blackmail."

"Yes! I'm stuck, Edmond. What do I do?"

"You love my sister? Do you swear it?"

"I swear on all that is holy, I do. But I'd rather lose her than have her disgraced. She still believes in all this one true faith mythology!"

"I know," I said. "We must all find a way to get out, and soon. Tell Anne that she is correct, that you have heard us plotting and we intend to ensnare Henry with Elizabeth and draw him from her side. She'll believe it; his love for her has already grown cold."

"How do I get out? Go home to Joan?"

"I'll talk to Henry. We're close."

"*How* close?"

I left the booth with Ursula still sitting there. I had to get an encrypted message off to my sister as quickly as possible.

～

As we waited for clarity, it became impossible to avoid court intrigue. Early one evening during evensong, a young woman would not stop staring at my Elizabeth. Even worse, Wolsey, Anne Boleyn, and Ursula were also giving her the side-eye throughout the mass.

"Who is she?" I whispered in Elizabeth's ear. She'd noticed the woman.

She shrugged. "I don't know, but it can't be good. She hasn't taken her eyes off me the entire service!"

"No, I don't have a good feeling about her. Why don't you retire to bed early? I'll tell them you fell ill."

I waited through the long service for the woman to make her move. And she wasted no time getting to me.

"Bishop Gregory!" The mysterious woman had fought her way through the crowd to be by my side. "Soon to be Cardinal Gregory, I heard."

I turned to her. "Have we met? I do apologize, but I can't seem to recall?" She looked vaguely familiar, but remembering faces or names wasn't one of my strengths.

She crinkled her nose, the freckles fading as she blushed a deep crimson. "You *have* forgotten me!"

Her russet orange hair peaked from under her hood as she tilted her head, appraising me.

Finally I shrugged, anxious for her to go. Cardinal Wolsey, Anne Boleyn, and Henry himself were making their way over to us—this curvy, ginger-hair was attracting attention, attention I didn't need.

I pulled at her elbow, moving her toward the door. "Do please remind me, my lady?"

"That night in Cambridge, silly! There were four of you, and we all drank far too much ale and ended up quite naked and unholy above the tavern, do you remember the—"

I pulled her harder, through the door and into the long hallway. I didn't remember her, or the night she referenced, but it was entirely possible. My early days in seminary had certainly been wild beyond memory.

"Of course," I lied. "But now, well, certainly things are far different."

She stared at me, her hands on her hips. "Are they, now?"

I nodded, turning to leave. She was growing tiresome, and I wanted to be with Elizabeth.

Her lips pressed into my ear. "I've heard that you are quite involved with a nun."

My face whipped toward her. "You dare accuse me?"

She nodded, a wicked smile across her lips. "I do dare, Father. And further, I happen to know that Tess Darby is not really a nun."

All color drained from my face at those two words: Tess Darby.

Her hand went to mine as we walked down the long gallery, away from the throng of courtiers. "Relax, Father," she said as we walked. "Of course your secret is safe with me! We are old friends, are we not?"

I gulped, waiting for her to show her cards.

"What is it that you want, Lady...?"

"Montfort. Lady Montfort, I am now but you can call me Kitty. It was so very difficult to convince my husband to bring me to court, but here we are!"

"Kitty, what is it you want?"

She laughed dramatically, throwing her head back as if she'd heard the most humorous thing ever. "I want *you*, Edmond!"

How much does she really know? I wondered. I had to find out.

"Kitty, is your husband otherwise occupied at this hour?" Out of view of the court, I wrapped my arm around her waist.

"Quite occupied! Do you have someplace discreet we might go to discuss these issues further?"

I walked her to my private rooms and barred the door behind us. We didn't make it past the outer sitting room before her body was all over mine.

"Edmond, I promise, I won't say a word about Tess Darby

of Worthington being here at court, being with you, after she was supposed to be killed in a fire. A fire that killed her husband! I won't mention to the new Queen Anne or His Majesty that I heard that her husband was quite a foul man, and that rumor around the village was that she was having a torrid affair with her confessor. That would be *you*, would it not?"

Her eyes narrowed as her hands groped at my waist, and below.

"Ah Kitty, such silly rumors. It would be a huge mistake to repeat such lies."

"Mm hm," she moaned, grinding her body against me in a crude, repulsive way. The woman had no skills in the art of seduction. I pitied her husband.

I pressed my member into her torso, and leaned in so that my lips were nearly touching hers. "What tavern was it in Cambridge? Where we met? I really want to recall that blissful night."

"I don't remember," she said, struggling to strip me of my heavy tunic. I took the robes off myself, until I was standing in front of her in only the leather trousers I'd worn underneath.

"Was I not with my best mate, George Townsend, the poet, during that time?" I asked, unlacing her heavy dress.

She reached up and removed her hood and shook her hair free. Her pale eyes were full of lust, and she struggled to maintain her composure.

"Oh yes! That's right. He was quite the lover, but none matched your vigor that night." Satisfied that she'd convinced me, she clawed at my bare chest with her nails as if a desperate cat in heat.

"Indeed," I said, turning her around and freeing her breasts. *Indeed,* I thought to myself. There was no George Townsend; I'd just made him up.

"Have you told your husband any of this?"

"Oh no," she said with a hard shake of her head. "That ancient fool would never understand. I only married him to be able to get close to you."

"I see."

"Oh Edmond, we shall be lovers! Secret lovers. And as long as we are in love, I shall not say anything to your superiors or the Lord Montfort about our trysts, *or* about Tess Darby." She said my love's name as if it were a curse, hatred oozing from her pursed lips.

"Of course," I said, my hands skating up her freckled skin toward her small breasts. She gasped; I was sure they'd never been touched before.

"And, my dearest, what shall we do about *Sister Elizabeth*?"

"She will have to go," she said in a moan, my fingertips working her into frenzy.

"So sensitive," I moaned in her ear.

"Yes," she said, her knees buckling as I stroked her pebble-hard nipples.

"How did you recognize her? You are very clever to see through our little deception."

I let one hand slip lower, into her skirts, hovering over her very sex itself. She pressed her hips forward, begging for more. *Not yet*, I thought.

"Kitty? Answer me."

"Ah," she groaned again, desperate for more. "I, uh, I followed you there. Watched you..."

I let a finger rest inside her, just shy of the throbbing place that would drive her to ecstasy. "Why do I not remember you?"

"I hid," she panted. "Don't be angry, Edmond! I've been in love with you for years. You never looked twice at me, but I had to know."

"Of course," I said gently, as if she'd just made the most

ordinary confession in the world. "Of course you did." I let my thumb slide into her quaking body.

"Kitty, that night in Cambridge—it never happened, did it?"

"No," she gasped, pressing her hips down in a desperate attempt for more of me. "But I wanted it to! I dreamt of it."

"I love another, though, Kitty. And you will do nothing to harm her, do you understand?" My left hand froze within her as my left wrapped around her long neck.

"I will tell! If you do not love me, then I will tell the entire nation. She is a murderer, Edmond. If I cannot have you, then she will die."

I took a deep breath and said, "As must you, poor troubled soul." My hand tightened on her neck. "Do you have anything you'd like to confess?"

"Edmond, I love you! You are mine."

My fingers left her quivering sex. My arms held her body still. I couldn't help but wish that there were another, less final, option. But this mad woman was dangerous, and would never cease her blackmail of me. She left me no choice.

As I gave her last rites, I commended her soul to heaven with a sudden twist of her neck. Her passing was quick and painless.

"Edmond!" A half-asleep Bess stared at me from the doorway of my inner bedchamber. Her eyes locked onto the dead corpse in my arms.

"See? Bloodless." I shrugged, letting the half-naked body of Kitty Montfort, or whoever she really was, slink to the ground.

"Easier to clean up, yes, but not nearly as much fun," she said, surveying my handiwork.

"I don't think anyone sent her. She seemed to be simply obsessed with me."

"So it seems." She walked over and stood above her. "Shall I dispose of her?"

I shook my head. "No, Bess, she needs to be buried."

"Buried!"

"She was insane. Wicked, but not right in her mind."

She laughed. "You read her last rites!"

I smiled back and shook my head. "Old habits I guess. But seriously, Bess, I didn't want to have to do that."

"I know. But burial is impossible."

"I sent her to the beyond, Elizabeth. The least I can do is let her rest in peace."

"Do you really believe all that?"

I shrugged. "No, I don't, but what does it hurt? Just in case? At the end, I was sort of her priest, after all."

"You are a wonderful man," she said, walking over to the window.

"The wonderful cleric who breaks your neck while stroking you off — I'm sure someday that'll be grounds for sainthood."

"Let it go, my love, and let's get rid of her. It's dark outside, perhaps a swim in the Thames?"

"No," I argued. "I'm serious about burial."

She took a deep breath. "Okay then, who gets to ask the king?"

"Elizabeth, I'll handle the disposal, but I need for you to grant me a slight," I searched my mind for the right word. "Dispensation."

"You need me to piece her out?"

I cringed. "God no, but you are a brutal little butcher, aren't you? No, I need to you to let me have a little leeway with Henry."

"Physical leeway?"

"Just a little. I may need to get him into an agreeable state before I make my request."

Her eyes narrowed. "Do what you need to, Edmond. This happened because of me, didn't it? You were keeping me safe."

"Partially. It was me she was after, but seeing you in Worthington gave her the fuel to finally act on her madness."

She gathered up her tunic and hood and headed toward the door. "Come to me later? Please don't sleep in the same room with this dead body."

I nodded. "I promise."

That night, after stuffing the corpse into a large crate, I washed my hands and made my way to Henry's private apartments.

Two guards stood at the inner door, where Henry slept. I walked over to the Groom of the Stool, the servant who knew the king's most private business. "William, is Henry, er, occupied this evening?"

He put his hand on my shoulder. William and I were friendly, and his position, though lowly in title, was that most close to the king himself. "He'd love to see you, I'm sure. The Queen is in there now, but from the sound of it, she won't be for long." He shot me a wink.

"She's not queen," I whispered. I refused to give in to her being given that title. To me, she was the king's mistress and nothing more. His wife lived, and Rome's refusal to grant an annulment was what started this whole plot to rid England of its errant monarch.

"You know we're in agreement on that, Edmond, but they insist."

We were interrupted by a massive bang from the other side of the king's great door. Both guards ran in, and we all saw Anne, her dress disheveled, with a great tankard in her hand. "The next one hits you, Henry!"

The guards quickly relieved her of her weapon and stood

in front of Henry, barely able to hold him off of her. "Get out, wench! Go from my presence!"

"Gladly! You smell bad tonight, my husband." With her skirts in hand, she ran from the room, at least five courtiers chasing after her.

Henry took a deep breath to calm himself before wiping blood from his lip. "She bit me, Edmond! Like a wild animal."

"Fiery indeed, Your Majesty," I said, fighting laughter.

"She missed me anyway. Catherine had a better arm – that crazy Spaniard would have made that shot."

I nodded remembering Catherine, Henry's true Queen. She bore her mother's courage, but would never have let the argument become public. "Lady Boleyn should rest if she is indeed with child, Harry. Caterwauling in your apartments is probably not what the medics want."

He sighed and hurled himself onto his great bed. "She keeps saying there's a boy inside her, but her belly has not grown in months."

"Has she had her monthly courses?"

He shrugged. "Who knows, I rarely touch her anymore. She bores me."

"Henry, I know the timing is bad, but I have to beg for a few minutes of your time. Privately?"

He patted at the giant fur blanket he was sitting on. "Always a few moments to spare for my dear friend. Sit."

With the wave of his hand, he cleared the room. "What can I do for you, my friend?"

"Oh, so much," I said with a wink, licking my lips.

"Now that's more like it!" He laughed his iconic belly laugh, and I couldn't help but laugh with him. It was contagious.

"But, alas, I can't give you a son!" I said through bouts of laughter, barely able to pronounce the words.

"No! Your arse is far too tight!"

At that we burst out, unable to maintain decorum. I needed him loose, in a good mood. When the laughter died down, I placed my hand on his inner thigh and leaned in. "You have to be the most enigmatic king in Christendom, Harry." With Henry, flattery would get you *everywhere*.

"You tease me, sweet Edmond."

I let my hand drift higher. "Truly I do not. There is no one like you." It wasn't a lie; he truly was an original. Leaning in to kiss him, I let him linger across my lips for several moments until I pulled back dramatically.

"I can't right now, sire. I'm sorry – I'm quite upset this evening."

He placed his large hand over mine, letting me lie back into the fluffy pillows. "So you really *did* want to talk." Disappointment dripped from his voice.

"Not *want* to, *have* to. But perhaps, after that, if you forgive me my sins, we can enjoy some private time."

His smile returned. "And Sister Elizabeth? Will she be joining us?"

"She's not feeling well today." He looked concerned. "Oh, nothing serious," I said quickly. "I suspect feminine issues. But she's tired, and bid me to come see you for the both of us."

His hand roamed across my trousers as he asked, "What sin have you committed, Father?"

"I can't have Elizabeth or my uncle, the Bishop, ever find out. Promise me, Harry?" I put my lips on his neck, hopeful that he'd be turned on enough to not be angry.

"I promise, I promise." He gave a quick squeeze to my thigh.

"Do you know the Lady Montfort?"

"Ah, I did hear she was here asking about you."

"We knew each other *quite* well in Cambridge."

He perked up. Harry loved a lascivious story. "She doesn't seem your type!"

"Wasn't, no, but I'm simply a man."

"Continue," he urged.

"After evensong she came to my rooms. Elizabeth was ill, and...well things progressed as they should not have."

His large hand gave me another jovial squeeze. "Do not worry, Edmond, a little dalliance in the court is acceptable, even for a cleric."

"It's more than that. She...this is quite embarrassing."

"You can tell me anything, Edmond."

"Lady Montfort engages in a quite perverted form of intercourse that involves her being choked. I'd never heard of such a thing," I lied.

He tilted his head, his eyes on fire. "Oh, Edmond, you are so naïve! It can be beyond erotic when done right!"

"Well," I said with a grimace, "It appears it was not done right."

He threw his head back to the mahogany headboard. "Oh, Edmond! How bad is it? Did you harm her?"

"She encouraged me, Majesty! She kept saying more, more, harder, harder. I-I'm not sure what went wrong but after our...our completion to ecstasy...she didn't wake up."

Barrel chest heaving, I could tell he wasn't sure whether to be angry or to laugh at my sexual incompetence. "Edmond, Edmond."

I leaned in to him, putting my head on his chest like a scolded dog. "I'm so sorry, Harry. Whatever will I do? Bess will leave me! I fear you shall never speak to me again."

"Oh Edmond, soft-hearted Edmond. Lord Montfort was seeking to put her away in a nunnery anyway. Just yesterday he petitioned the court on grounds of insanity."

"I do think she was mad," I said, praying he was buying the story.

"Positively senile."

"How will I get out of this? You are so much wiser than me, please give me counsel."

More flattery. And he fell for it without a second thought. "Leave it to me, my love. Where is the dearly departed now?"

"In a trunk in my chambers. The black one."

He nodded. "Think on this no more." His hand gave my most delicate place a squeeze as he rolled over toward me.

"Oh, and I think Sister Ursula might have seen more than she should have."

"Shall we take care of her, too?"

My fingers skated up his massive, muscled thigh. "No, if you could just arrange to have her sent back to Cambridge? My sister has further need of her."

"Done," he said as he untied my trousers.

ELIZABETH

I was fast asleep when Edmond crawled into my bed the night prior. He mumbled something about the king before pulling me close and falling fast asleep. When I woke, he was gone.

That morning as I walked to mass, the court was in a flutter. Whispers, looks, swishes of skirts, snickers of men – there was drama. But then again, it was the Tudor court of the still-young King Henry the Eighth, and there was *always* drama.

"Did you hear?" A novice nun nearly howled from the door as I rounded the corner. *I so wished I'd seen Edmond that morning!*

"No, what's going on, Sister Ruth?"

"Lady Montfort fell her to her death last night!"

"Oh my heavens!" I made the sign of the cross.

"She was acting insane all day! But no one expected *that*!"

"I didn't know her. Do they know what happened?"

"She was found soaked in wine. It is said she either stumbled out of the window, or..." Sister Ruth made a quick sign of the cross.

"Or?" I asked.

"Well, her husband petitioned the court to have her put away. Some say that Lady Montfort jumped out of the window. Her neck was broken."

"A tragedy," I said, turning to walk into the chapel.

It wasn't until halfway through mass when I finally was able to talk to Edmond. "Well done," I said into his ear.

Clearly exhausted, he tilted his head back. The dark spiral curls I adored fell back across his shoulders. "Let's pray they all believe it."

"Henry?"

"Henry believed the tale of my sexual impropriety."

I bumped him with my shoulder. "How could one believe such a thing of innocent Father Gregory?" I teased.

~

Barely able to breathe from one scandal of the court, another quickly reared its head. Later that very day, it was hard to miss him. The red cardinal robes swishing as he walked with a purpose. Cardinal Wolsey *always* walked with a purpose. "Sister may we speak?"

He stood in front of me, impatiently shifting from one ruby slipper to the next. "Of course, Your Eminence."

I waited for him to speak, knowing that he couldn't possibly have any good reason to approach me. He cleared his throat and began. "It would seem Sister Ursula has been taken to the Tower."

That I did not expect. My hand flew to my mouth in a momentary betrayal of emotion. "Has she been arrested?"

"She's been taken in for questioning."

Edmond walked up behind me. "As in torture?"

"As in questioning," Wolsey answered.

"And you're telling us, so I'm guessing you are not behind this?" I asked.

The edges of his lips curled up in a sneer. "If I were, Sister, then why would I be standing here informing you?"

Edmond put a hand on my shoulder. "Well then, do you know what it's about?"

He shook his head. "I don't, and Henry doesn't seem to either."

"If the king doesn't know, then it had to have been Anne." Edmond glanced around the empty sanctuary, ensuring there were no listening ears.

"Listen, we're on the same side, somewhat. Like you, *Bishop* Gregory, I have no desire to break with Rome," Wolsey said.

I knew Edmond gave no care to his ecclesiastical position, but his uncle had the same hopes for the papacy that Wolsey did.

"What is it you want from us?" I asked.

He looked around the room again before answering. In a barely audible whisper, he said the six words that made sweat break out on the back of my neck.

"I want you to kill her."

We both stared at him, incredulous.

"Kill Anne Boleyn? No." Edmond crossed his arms in front of himself, glaring at Wolsey.

"I've heard Sister Elizabeth is quite skilled at such things. There's a rumor, in fact, that she was sent here by Reginald Gregory to do such a thing to our own beloved monarch. Now, when I heard such things of course I dispelled of these wild notions."

He was threatening us.

"I can help you afterward, get you out. But if she is gone, the king will return to his wife and the one true church."

Edmond took a deep breath before answering. "It's not

that simple, Cardinal. If Anne is gone, he'll seek another. And another after her. Henry is not going to stop this madness until he is borne a son. Doing away with Anne is pointless. Besides, he says she's with child."

Wolsey let out an uncharacteristic chuckle. "Lunacy! She's right now having her monthly courses."

I had to ask. "How do you know that?"

"I have eyes and ears everywhere. Everywhere! That is how I knew of your plot and also of your talents. Some would call such gifts the two of you possess witchcraft."

I instinctively crossed myself, as if I could use some ancient ritual to ward off the evil we were entrenched in. "I could not do such a thing."

Wolsey snorted, clearly not pleased. "You will, and you'll do it within the next few days. If you do not, I shall be forced to present evidence of your treachery to the king."

"You have no evidence, Your Eminence. The charge is false, and Henry will see through it."

"You may have his bed," the cardinal spat. "But I have his ear!"

"There has to be another way," I said in desperation.

"There is not!" he nearly shouted. In a huff, he turned and left us in the same red whirlwind that he'd arrived in.

❧

"So what do we do?" I asked.

Edmond sat across from me at my small dining table, our dinner growing cold between us. "It's time for our end game. Let's hope he loves us."

"We have to get Ursula home."

"Look at you, all soft-hearted."

"No, never. It's just…"

"Seriously. Soft-hearted," he teased.

I tossed a piece of bread at him, hitting him square in the nose. "Mature," he laughed.

I dipped my spoon into the tepid soup. "Who can we trust?"

"No one," he answered.

"Surely Henry loves you enough to save you."

"Save us. And he loves us. But, my love, when this explodes, he's going to question that love. If I were him, I'd wonder if our affections were false, part of a plot."

I nodded. "Yes. And for me, that is how they began."

He gnawed at the crust of bread, deep in thought. "I'm going to beg the king to free her. When she is safely home, I'll tell him everything."

"Let's hope we have that kind of time." I dipped a piece of bread into my soup as a plan of my own hatched in my impetuous head.

~

Edmond may have made his peace with Ursula, but I had not. Not yet.

Early the next morning, I slipped out of the palace gates and joined the throngs of city dwellers making their way through the sewage-filled streets of London. I knew getting to the Tower would be easy, but getting inside would be a challenge.

Sneaking in wasn't an option; at least not in the traditional way. I decided instead to take an enormous gamble and practice a new skill Edmond had been teaching me during our endless hours at court. A skill, I was fully aware, that I had yet to actually get to work.

At the gates, I looked for the most amenable guard I could find. A knot formed in my stomach when I realized the guard I must choose from experiment was the biggest, most burly one of the bunch. And due to the sheer number of them, my dagger would be pretty much useless.

I got his attention by placing my hand on his sleeve. He startled, completely aware of my presence. I took that as a good sign – he wasn't particularly bright.

"Oh good sir, I apologize. I'm a bit lost." I stared into his dark eyes, my mind speaking to him in ways my lips did not. *I am to be trusted,* I thought over and over again. "Believe the words yourself!" I could hear Edmond say, as he'd scolded me countless times in practice.

"Lost?" The guard's eyes were locked onto mine.

"I was sent by Cardinal Wolsey himself to pray with a sister who is here."

"Cardinal…" he repeated. *She is telling the truth, you must help her,* my mind said, over and over and over until he spoke again.

"Need help," he finally said. His mind was weak. I'd been lucky that I chose well.

"You are to help me speak to Sister Ursula Houston." *Take her, take her, take her,* my thoughts screamed at the man.

"Take you," he grumbled.

As he headed into the ominous gates, I followed.

"Say nothing," I said out loud to him, his back to me. *Say nothing, tell no one,* my thoughts told him.

"Tell no one," he repeated out loud. I had him, but I also knew that my concentration was weak, and that at any time the spell could be broken.

After several long corridors, the thump of his boots echoing through the passages, we arrived at a chamber door. "Other guards are at mass," he mumbled, opening the heavy wooden door with a large iron key.

"I'll only be a short while."

"Short while," he repeated. "Tell no one."

Ursula sat in a wooden chair at a small window in the corner. "Wait for me, Horatio."

As he closed the door, leaving us alone, he said, "Tell no one. Wait."

"Black magic!" Ursula said from her chair.

"No, just a strong mind versus a weak one."

She glared at me. "I left that witchcraft long ago."

"I heard," I said, sitting down across from her. "That it left you."

"Why are you here? I've told them nothing!"

I leaned in to look at her in the faint glow of the candle-light. Her face was bruised, a chunk of hair missing, and a finger was wrapped in cloth. "Did they torture you?"

"Not really. Some rough questioning, but I think they are afraid to truly harm a woman of the cloth."

"Anne Boleyn is the one who brought you here."

She nodded. "As I thought. She will let me rot in here."

"Edmond is going to ask the king to release you. When he does, you must go back to the abbey, to Joan. Leave everything and get out of London."

She took a drink of water. "Are you going to do it?"

"I don't know," I answered. At that moment, I wasn't sure exactly what my future held. "But if he can get you out, you *must* run."

She smiled at me. "I will."

I rose to leave. "Elizabeth," she said. "Thank you. I thought you had come to kill me, to silence me."

"I wouldn't do that to Joan. But Ursula, don't make me regret it."

The monolithic guard, Horatio, walked me back to the gates. Once more, I reminded him, "Say nothing."

"Say nothing," he said as he walked back to his post.

Getting into the Tower was far easier than I'd expected, and I felt a wave of hope for the first time in days. My skills were improving, and surely we were about to go home.

And then his eyes locked with mine.

From a foul smelling market stall, Jacob the Tanner saw me. My first instinct was to run, but if I did that, I risked him talking. No one could know that I was alive.

Be brave. With that chant in my head, I approached Jacob. Slowly, as if nothing was wrong, I made my way through the crowd and to his stall. The stench was almost more than I could bear, with the cowhides in various states of decay, and the contaminated water flowing from his work. Flowing straight into the city's water supply, I couldn't help but notice.

"Jacob, kind sir! It is so good to see you."

His eyes were wide, as if he'd seen a ghost. Wiping his red-stained hands on a cloth, he walked closer to me. "Tess?"

Inside, I felt as if I'd be ill. But outside, my demeanor was as if I'd just run into him a year earlier in the market in Worthington. "Yes!" I said with a smile. "Fancy seeing you in London Town."

He smiled back, the puzzled look never leaving him. "Tess," he said again. "You're supposed to be dead. I went to your funeral."

I nodded. "I can explain."

He gestured toward the back of his stall, where a heavy curtain blocked the view from the public. "Can you sit a spell?"

I sat on a tiny three-legged stool in the corner. He knelt close to me on the bloody ground. "Please don't tell anyone, Jacob. I had to do what I did."

"Did you...? Some say you killed both your father and John the Brewer."

I shook my head vigorously. "Lies! That is why I had to run."

He smiled and exhaled a deep breath. "I knew you would *never* do such a thing. You are good, Tess."

I took his stained hand and leaned in close. "I did make a mistake. One night I confessed to my wicked husband that I loved another."

He pulled his hand away. "I knew you were in love with the priest. We all did."

"Oh no!" I said, reaching for his hand again. "Heavens no."

He looked puzzled. "Then...who?"

I brought my face as close to his as I dared. "I was in love with you."

"With me!" He smiled so wide I thought his blood-smeared face would crack.

I winked at him. "I do wish things had worked out differently, Jacob."

"And now you are married to God," he said, a wave of disappointment washing over him.

"I'm afraid so, yes. It was the only way to atone for loving another. And when the fire happened, I knew it was God telling me to repent. Of course those in the village would never believe me."

"No, no," he said. "They would not. They tried to burn your mother as a witch!"

I acted shocked. "That is horrid! My mother was a God-fearing woman. It was Father who..." I trailed off, letting Jacob's mind fill in the blanks.

"Yes, I thought all along he was the one with the potions."

"She always liked you," I said, rising as if to go.

"And I her. But I was barely over your death when she suggested that I marry her."

My own mother, that man-hunter, I thought.

"Jacob, I must go, but if you are able to find happiness with my mother, I give you my blessing. For eternity, I must stay chaste before our Lord. But, Jacob Tanner, I will forever carry you in my heart."

"Godspeed to you, Tess."

"And to you."

I left, walking at a casual pace back to the palace. I could only hope that Jacob would stay silent, but I did hope he might eventually tell my mother of our meeting.

When I made it back to my chambers, Edmond leapt out from behind the door.

"I have been worried."

"Seriously worried?" I teased.

"Bess, please don't do that again. They told me you went into the city, alone."

I held up my tannin stained palms. "I guess you caught me red-handed."

"Humorous," he said. "Wait, why were you buying leather goods?"

"No I went to see Ursula. And then, on the way home, Jacob the Tanner spied me."

His mouth fell open. "Oh no! In a city of so many, the odds of that. We are truly doomed."

"No, my love, we have only just begun. See Henry, do what you must. It's time for us to fly away, one way or another."

EDMOND

*A*fter the wine was poured, I asked to be alone with Henry. With a lusty grin, he cleared the room so that we were fully alone.

"Is it to be just us tonight, Edmond? Has our skillful little bird grown tired of us?"

His hand reached from his manhood as I shook my head. "Harry, I have to tell you the entire truth. I wish there was another way, but I fear that Bess and I are out of options."

His face grew white, the mood in the room forever changed. I knew at that moment we'd never again be lovers.

"Speak freely," he barked.

"You're correct, as usual. Elizabeth is indeed not my cousin, or even truly Elizabeth at all."

"I knew that." He slammed his heavy tankard on the small table between us.

I took a deep breath. Henry was losing his patience, and an angry King Henry was a very dangerous thing indeed.

"What happened to the real Elizabeth Gregory?" he asked.

"Suicide, they say. She became pregnant with the child of

one of the cooks in her father's kitchen. Not only was she a nun, but she dared to fornicate with a servant."

"Stupid girl."

"They covered it up, saying only that she'd gone overseas to a nunnery. It was easy enough to bring my beloved into the identity that was vacated."

"I was once your beloved."

I looked away. He had no idea how much worse it was about to get.

"You were, and I will always love you. But she is my life, my soul, the very breath in my lungs. Elizabeth is everything to me."

"Let's hope she lives longer than the *other* Elizabeth."

I tried to ignore the threatening tone in his voice. "She was sent here to kill you."

A look of disbelief clouded his face, followed by the red blush of an angry Henry.

He thundered up from his chair, knocking the table and our wine to the floor. "Edmond Gregory, do you dare come to my private chamber and confess a plot of treason against me?"

"Well, I take it you *hadn't* heard then."

"You had best be very careful, sir!" he raged. His giant hand wrapped around my neck, dragging me to his body. "You knew this all along?"

"Yes. I told you the first day that I came to protect you."

"I shall slice her head open!"

"You won't," I said calmly.

"What makes you so sure?"

"Because I love her as you love her. And you love me."

He released the grip on my neck. "As if love was enough. What a fallacy! Go, get out of my sight."

"Love is always enough, Harry."

I walked to the door, waiting for him to stop me, but he did not.

ELIZABETH

"Well, what happened?" I asked anxiously. Edmond had been gone nearly an hour, an hour alone with Henry.

"He listened. I told him everything."

"And?" I pulled at his collar, forcing him to look me in the eye.

"And I don't know, Bess. He collapsed into his bed, pulled the covers over his head, and commanded me from the room."

And so we waited, but nothing happened. We conducted services as normal in the chapel and retired to bed together as we always had. What we didn't know was that our shared bedchamber no longer had the king's protection.

In the middle of the night, the door was forced open.

Twenty guards marched in and pulled me from our bed. I naturally began to fight until Edmond reached for me. "It's no use, Bess. We are undone."

Allowed to dress, we were taken to the Tower by boat. I shuddered under my heavy robes as we passed under the

Traitor's Gate. Most sent to the Tower by the Tudors never returned.

Edmond held my hand, his face calm.

"Will he kill us?" I asked

"Maybe, or worse. I took a gamble, we all did. We shall see."

~

We spent three days in the Tower. Our room was cozy, not the stone cell that I envisioned. Truly our shared room, unheard of in itself, was even nicer than my rooms at the palace.

Each of those three dark nights I clung to Edmond, willing myself to be strong.

On the third day, we were charged with Unlawful Carnal Knowledge. When the guard left, Edmond smiled.

"What? You seem relieved."

He nodded at me. "What *weren't* we charged with?"

I wrapped myself around him, the answer to his question bouncing in my head. We were *not* charged with treason.

Late that night, the massive form of our Henry woke us. He took me into his powerful arms and twirled me around the room as he did during our first few days together.

"Hush, my falcon. The guards mustn't hear," he warned.

"I never would have done it! I swear to you, Your Majesty."

He kissed me on the cheek. "You *should* have done it. The world would have been a much more peaceful place if you'd taken my life at the very beginning. We should not have shared the love that we did, we three."

Edmond's eyes locked with Henry's. "It's over. Isn't it, Harry?"

The larger-than-life king nodded sadly. "Yes. There's no

other way. I've come to say my goodbyes."

I felt a tear roll down my cheek, but I wiped it away. I would not show weakness in the face of the storm, only strength.

"I've arranged passage through France for the both of you," Henry said as if he were relaying the current weather.

"Will we ever return?" I thought of my mother, my family, our beloved dog, Beast. But most of all, I thought of the often joyous, intelligent, larger-than-life king that had become such a part of my world.

"No," Henry said.

"So you're banning me from your life once again," Edmond said.

"There's no other option, my darlings. I am a king, and you are outlaws."

"And what will come of you? Others will come. Will you give up on breaking with Rome?"

He shook his head. "No, my loves. I must follow my own path, no matter where it leads. And you must go."

I looked away from him—I knew he was right. We could stay and die as three, or flee so that we would live to fight another day. As much as it hurt, Henry had to stay and rule, marry and have an heir, form his own church no matter what the consequences. And we had to nurture the love of the three of us elsewhere, without him.

"So it's goodbye again, Harry," Edmond said.

"It must be. I will marry Anne and she will bear me a son. Finally, after all of the struggle, my father's throne will be secure."

"We'll write and you can come see us when you—"

Henry interrupted me with the raising of his oversized hand. "You are far too precious for me to lie to, my sweet girl. Contact of any sort is far too dangerous for all of us. You must disappear, sink quietly into your roles."

"I'll never forget you," I said.

"Nor will she ever be quiet," Edmond joked.

We shared a laugh; laughter through our tears. When the room grew quiet, Henry took me into his arms and lifted my off my feet in a final King Henry bear hug. "You must, powerful falcon, you must. I need you to love and take care of Edmond. I can't bear to think of the two of you not forever bound in blissful love."

He looked to Edmond. "Edmond, I love you, forever and always. Pray for me."

The three of us embraced one final time, clasping each other for what we knew would be the last time the three of us would ever be together.

A whistle from the river came far too quickly and it was time to go.

Henry looked to me. "There's a friar on the other side of the journey. You'll know him by his snowy white beard and his flesh will bear proof that he was sent to you by me."

"You made a deal with the devil?" Edmond smiled at Henry.

"Maybe, temporarily at least."

"And what of Sister Ursula?"

"She was freed days ago and sent back to your sister in Cambridge."

"Thank you for that," Edmond said.

"She mentioned a dog? I can send him on the next ship over."

Edmond shook his head. "He belongs to the orphanage now. They need him."

With one last touch of his hand, I said the ridiculous. "I'm sorry I tried to kill you."

"If you'd tried, I wouldn't be before you now. And mark my words, others will try, and they will keep trying. But none, my falcon, will ever be as skilled as yourself."

I kissed him, as did Edmond, before we were swept out into the night toward the ship Henry commissioned to take us to freedom. It would be decades before I saw him again.

~

It was a long journey, but thankfully smooth. I'd never been on the open sea before, and any wind tortured me with seasickness. When it was calm, I'd cling to my beloved Edmond. Our hearts broke at leaving our Henry, but we had each other and were determined to never part.

When the boat, one of the finest pirate ships to ever sail, landed at Calais we were greeted by the dark hooded figure of a monk. "Follow," he snapped.

Under cover of the darkest night, he led us to the monastery that would be our refuge for the next two years. Only when we were secured into our simple cell did he speak again.

"This was a huge risk," he said in a near growl, his Scottish brogue a surprise to me. When he pulled the cowl from around his head, the stark white of his hair and long beard glowed in the candlelight.

"Why then? Why take the chance to save two ghosts?" I asked.

He pulled up the heavy burlap sleeve of his tunic to reveal the white and red Tudor rose inked into his skin. "Because I love him, too."

We spent years in the service of the Friar. Later, when we were too old to live the life of intrigue, we retired to a quiet farm far away from the courts of Europe. I never bore children, as I knew I would not, but I spent a lifetime in love with my Edmond. It was years after the peaceful passing in his sleep that I was once again called upon to kill the king.

EPILOGUE: ELIZABETH

*T*here was one final role I was yet to play.

I was baking bread at my hearth when the messenger brought the letter. It bore a wax seal, imprinted with the King of England's own ring.

After so many years, it was finally time to complete my mission.

I slipped into the room unrecognized with the throng of priests and clergy. Wrapped in a monk's robe, my face hidden, no one looked at me twice. They were too focused on the dying king to bother.

As the commotion ensued, I slowly worked my way to his bedside.

I knelt next to the king. A massive form, his body wrecked by the unhealed wounds of his youth, this man was completely unrecognizable to me. The strong, vigorous man I'd once grown to love was no longer.

As he requested, I freed his soul from the hell he'd lived in for years. With the slip of my knife into his ribs, not a word left his mouth. His body felt hardly any pain, my jab so precise and quick. But his eyes...he looked at me. For a second, they weren't the cloudy eyes of a monolith, but instead the sparkling blue of the Henry I knew.

"With Edmond now," he said into my hooded ear. "I see him—young, beautiful, and waiting for you."

As he passed, the crowd clamored around him but I'd already slipped off into the night, exchanging my monk's robe for the beautiful gown I'd hidden in a nearby room.

It was over. I'd finally done the thing I was destined to do from the very beginning—killing the king.

FROM FINDING THE FRIAR, COMING
2019

"Forgive me Father, for I have sinned," he said from the other side of the iron screen.

"What sin have you committed, my brother?"

The hooded monk leaned in close. "Ah, Cardinal Gregory, it is dire. I tried to kill the Pope of Rome."

I leaned back, the grin on my lips betraying me. "Ah, Franco. I've missed you."

He laughed, that hard chuckle that only the Scottish can make sound jovial versus evil. Well, maybe a little bit evil when it came to Friar Franco.

~

Elizabeth:

It was warmer there, and the air drier. At sunrise, I looked out of our window, high atop a broad hill. The valley below was covered in yellow flowers, the sky azure blue. I never wanted to leave France.

"Beautiful girl," Edmond said from behind me. His chin rested on my bare shoulder as he joined me at the window.

"Who is he? The Friar? I thought he'd be French with a name like Franco, but he sounded Scottish."

His lips kissed my shoulder and his swelling member pressed into me. "Very much Scottish. Franco is a name we use to avoid ever revealing his true identity."

I turned to him, pressing my body into his. "And what is his true identity, my dear Edmond?"

He ground against me, our desire growing unbearable. "I do not know. Franco is a play on words in that is he is a monk of the Franciscan order. As far as who he is, we do not know. His identity must remain a secret."

"Hm, one who cannot be named." The idea intrigued me.

"Yes, a ghost."

"Like us!" My body melted into his as he led me back to bed.

"Well-sexed ghosts!"

Word-of-mouth is crucial for any author to succeed. If you enjoyed this book, please leave a review on Amazon. Even if it were just a sentence or two, it would make all the difference and would be very much appreciated.

ACKNOWLEDGMENTS

Killing the King was a glorious experiment in so many ways. I've never enjoyed writing a book as much as this one. Thank you to my readers who were willing to let me stretch out a bit and pursue a new kind of story.

To my family, as always, for putting up with the pain of the process and supporting me anyway.

To Carol Hall, Daphne Caldwell, and Kelly McKinnon for always being there to proofread my books.

And to my review team of twenty-one dedicated readers, you have made my day. Okay, my month. My year. Seriously, as Edmond would say, there are no words for how much I value my loyal group of word warriors. Thank you.

ABOUT THE AUTHOR

Sam JD Hunt resides in Las Vegas with her husband as well as her two children.

When not writing, Hunt enjoys travel, community involvement, spending time with friends and family, and hiking. She spends her days writing and trying to answer the age-old question: is it too late for coffee or too early for wine?

 facebook.com/SJDHunt

twitter.com/sjd_hunt

instagram.com/sjd_hunt